RAPUNZEL AND OTHER
Magic Fairy Tales

SELECTED AND ILLUSTRATED BY
HENRIETTE SAUVANT

TRANSLATED BY
ANTHEA BELL

EGMONT

Translator's Preface

The stories in this book of fairy tales, selected and illustrated by Henriette Sauvant, include some of the most famous ever told, like 'Cinderella' and 'Hansel and Gretel', and others that you may not have read before, such as 'The Sea Rabbit' and 'The Drummer'. They have all been around for a very long time, and no one knows how or when they were first told. What is certain is that they were passed on by word of mouth from one storyteller to another for centuries before anyone ever thought of writing them down. The story of 'Cinderella', for instance, exists in hundreds of versions all over the world. There is even a centuries-old Chinese version.

Fairy tales were not told especially for children in the first place. They appealed to adults as well, and they still do. We can tell from quotations in other written works that they existed far back in the past. So why was it so long before the stories were written down? The answer is simply that no one thought they were grand enough. Educated writers felt they were just old tales told by ordinary people and not worthy of print. Then, in the first half of the seventeenth century, an Italian called Giambattista Basile published the first collection of printed fairy tales. After that other people became interested in collecting and printing traditional tales, particularly the famous Grimm brothers, Jacob and Wilhelm, who published the first edition of their Children's and Household Tales in Germany in 1812–15. Most of the stories in this book are from the collection of the Grimms, who asked friends, family and acquaintances to tell them the stories they knew. One very useful source close to their home in Kassel was a tailor's widow in her sixties called Dorothea Viehmann, who regularly came to town to sell produce from her garden. She was an innkeeper's daughter, and as a girl had probably heard many stories told by visitors to her father's inn. Another storyteller was an old soldier called Johann Friedrich Krause. Other people who gave the Grimms stories were well-educated young women, one of them a family friend, Dorothea Wild, who married Wilhelm Grimm in 1823. Another contributor was Marie Hassenpflug, a friend of the Grimms' sister, Charlotte. As children, these young women had heard the old stories told by people who probably could not read or write, and now they helped the Grimms to record them for future readers.

Other collectors were also at work in Europe, and the version of 'Hansel and Gretel' that you will read here is from the German collector Ludwig Bechstein. 'Jack and the Beanstalk' is from an English collection made by Joseph Jacobs and published in 1890. All the other stories are translated from their best-known written versions. We hope you will enjoy them. You will find a few words about each story at the end of it.

 Contents

Rapunzel

Once upon a time a man and his wife had been longing to have a baby, but in vain. Then, at last, the woman thought that God was going to grant their wish.

The couple had a little window at the back of their house, and if they looked out of it they could see a wonderful garden full of the most beautiful flowers and herbs. However, it was surrounded by a high wall, and no one dared go in, because it belonged to a very powerful witch. Everyone feared her. One day the woman was standing at the window looking down into the garden, and she caught sight of a bed full of fine plants of lamb's lettuce or rapunzel. They looked so fresh and green that she longed to eat some of them. Her longing grew every day, and knowing that she couldn't have the lamb's lettuce she wasted away and looked pale and miserable.

Her husband was alarmed, and he asked, 'What's the matter, dear wife?'

'Oh,' she replied, 'if I don't get some of the lamb's lettuce from the garden behind our house to eat, I feel sure I shall die.'

The man loved his wife, and he thought, rather than let her die I must fetch her some of that lamb's lettuce at any price.

He climbed the wall of the witch's garden in the evening twilight, quickly picked a handful of the plants, and took them to his wife. She immediately made them into a salad and ate it with a hearty appetite. But the lamb's lettuce had tasted so good that she craved it three times as much next day. If she was to have any peace, her husband would have to climb into the garden again. So he set off in the evening twilight once more, but when he had climbed down from the wall he had a terrible fright, for there stood the witch.

'How dare you climb into my garden?' she said, with a furious glance at him. 'How dare you steal my lamb's lettuce? You'll be sorry for this.'

'Please have mercy!' said the man. 'I did it only because I had to: my wife has seen your lamb's lettuce from our window, and longs to eat it so much that she'll die if she doesn't get some.'

Then the witch's anger died down, and she told him, 'In that case you may take as much lamb's lettuce as you like, but on one condition: when your wife has her baby you must give it to me. The child will be well off, and I'll care for it like a mother.' In his fear, the man agreed, and as soon as his wife had her baby the witch appeared, called the child Rapunzel, and took the little girl away with her.

Rapunzel was the prettiest child ever seen. When she was twelve years old the witch shut her up in a tower in the middle of a forest. It had no stairs or doors, only one little window very high up on the walls. When the witch wanted to come in, she stood at the bottom of the tower and called:

'Rapunzel, Rapunzel,
Let down your hair.'

Rapunzel had beautiful long hair, as fine as spun gold, and when she heard the witch's voice she undid her braids, wound her hair around a hook in the window frame, and let it fall twenty feet to the ground so that the witch could climb up it.

After a few years the king's son happened to be riding through the forest, and he rode past the tower. He heard such a lovely song inside that he stopped to listen. It was Rapunzel, amusing herself in her loneliness by singing in her sweet voice.

The prince wanted to climb up to her, and looked for a door in the tower, but there was none to be found. He rode home, but the song had moved him so deeply that he went out into the forest every day to hear it. One day, as he was standing behind a tree, he saw the witch coming and heard her call up:

'Rapunzel, Rapunzel,
Let down your hair.'

The girl's long hair dropped from the window, and the witch climbed up it. If that's the way into the tower, the prince thought, then I'll try my own luck. And next day at twilight he went to the tower and called:

'Rapunzel, Rapunzel,
Let down your hair.'

The hair immediately fell from the window, and the prince climbed up it. At first Rapunzel was scared to death when he came in, for she had never seen a man before, but the prince began talking to her gently, telling her how her singing had moved his heart so much that it gave him no rest, and he had to see her for himself. Now Rapunzel wasn't frightened any more, and when the prince asked if she would marry him, and she saw how young and handsome he was, she thought, he'll be kinder to me than my old godmother the witch. So she agreed and put her hand in his.

'I'll go with you happily,' she said, 'but I don't know how to get down to the ground. If you bring me a skein of silk every time you come to see me, I'll weave the silk into a ladder, and when it's ready I'll climb down and you can take me up on your horse.'

They agreed that he would visit her every evening until then, because the old witch came in the daytime. The witch noticed nothing until one day Rapunzel said to her, 'Tell me, Godmother, why are you so much heavier to pull up than the king's young son? He climbs up here in the twinkling of an eye.'

'Oh, you wicked child,' cried the witch. 'What's this I hear? I thought I'd kept you well away from the rest of the world, but you've deceived me!'

She was so angry that she seized Rapunzel's beautiful hair, wound it a couple of times around her left hand, took a pair of scissors in her right hand, and snip, snap, off came the hair and the beautiful braids lay on the floor. Showing no mercy, she took poor Rapunzel to a wilderness where she had to live in great misery and want.

On the evening of the day when she had carried Rapunzel away to the wilderness, the witch fastened the braids she had cut off to the hook in the window frame, and when the prince came along and called:

'*Rapunzel, Rapunzel,*
Let down your hair,'

she let the hair drop. The king's son climbed it, but at the top of the tower he found not his beloved Rapunzel but the witch, who looked at him venomously.

'Aha,' she said scornfully, 'so you've come for your dear wife, but the pretty bird has flown the nest and won't sing any more. And the cat who caught the bird will scratch your eyes out too. You've lost Rapunzel, and you'll never see her again.'

The king's son was beside himself with grief, and in his despair he jumped out of the tower window. He escaped with his life, but he fell into some thorns which put his eyes out, blinding him. Then he wandered around the forest, eating nothing but roots and berries, and weeping and wailing for the loss of his beloved wife. So he wandered around in misery for several years, and at last he came to the wilderness where Rapunzel was scraping a living with the twin children she had borne him, a boy and a girl. He heard a voice, and it seemed to him very familiar, so he followed it. When he came closer Rapunzel recognised him, flung her arms around his neck and wept. Two of her tears fell on his eyes, his eyesight was restored, and he could see as well as ever. He took Rapunzel to his kingdom, where he was welcomed back with joy, and they lived happily together for many years to come.

Translator's note: The name of the famous long-haired heroine of this well-known tale is a German word for more than one kind of plant, and has become familiar in English through this story. But exactly what plant did the Grimms mean? One of their many projects was compiling a huge dictionary of the German language, and in it we find that they listed the scientific Latin names of several plants under the word 'Rapunzel': including a species of bell-flower called 'rampion' in English, and the 'lamb's lettuce' still widely eaten today as a salad herb (chosen for this translation).

A common theme in fairy tales is the bargain struck with a human who trespasses on the property of a witch or fairy, demanding an unborn child in return for sparing the intruder.

The Grimms took as the basis of this story a French version of a story in the Italian first-ever collection of fairy tales mentioned in the Preface.

Jack and the Beanstalk

There was once upon a time a poor widow who had an only son named Jack, and a cow named Milky-white. And all they had to live on was the milk the cow gave every morning, which they carried to the market and sold. But one morning Milky-white gave no milk, and they didn't know what to do.

'What shall we do, what shall we do?' said the widow, wringing her hands.

'Cheer up, mother, I'll go and get work somewhere,' said Jack.

'We've tried that before, and nobody would take you,' said his mother; 'we must sell Milky-white and with the money start a shop, or something.'

'All right, mother,' says Jack; 'it's market-day today, and I'll soon sell Milky-white, and then we'll see what we can do.'

So he took the cow's halter in his hand, and off he started. He hadn't gone far when he met a funny-looking old man, who said to him: 'Good morning, Jack.'

'Good morning to you,' said Jack, and wondered how he knew his name.

'Well, Jack, and where are you off to?' said the man.

'I'm going to market to sell our cow there.'

'Oh, you look the proper sort of chap to sell cows,' said the man; 'I wonder if you know how many beans make five.'

'Two in each hand and one in your mouth,' says Jack, as sharp as a needle.

'Right you are,' says the man, 'and here they are, the very beans themselves,' he went on, pulling out of his pocket a number of strange-looking beans. 'As you are so sharp,' says he, 'I don't mind doing a swap with you – your cow for these beans.'

'Go along,' said Jack; 'wouldn't you like it?'

'Ah! you don't know what these beans are,' said the man; 'if you plant them overnight, by morning they grow right up to the sky.'

'Really?' said Jack; 'you don't say so.'

'Yes, that is so, and if it doesn't turn out to be true you can have your cow back.'

'Right,' says Jack, and hands him over Milky-white's halter and pockets the beans.

Back goes Jack home, and as he hadn't gone very far it wasn't dusk by the time he got to his door.

'Back already, Jack?' said his mother; 'I see you haven't got Milky-white, so you've sold her. How much did you get for her?'

'You'll never guess, mother,' says Jack.

'No, you don't say so. Good boy! Five pounds, ten, fifteen, no, it can't be twenty.'

'I told you you couldn't guess. What do you say to these beans; they're magical, plant them overnight and – '

'What!' says Jack's mother, 'have you been such a fool, such a dolt, such an idiot, as to give away my Milky-white, the best milker in the parish, and prime beef to boot, for a set of paltry beans? Take that! Take that! Take that! And as for your precious beans here they go out of the window. And now off with you to bed. Not a sup shall you drink, and not a bit shall you swallow this very night.'

So Jack went upstairs to his little room in the attic, and sad and sorry he was, to be sure, as much for his mother's sake, as for the loss of his supper.

At last he dropped off to sleep.

When he woke up, the room looked so funny. The sun was shining into part of it, and yet all the rest was quite dark and shady. So Jack jumped up and dressed himself and went to the window. And what do you think he saw? Why, the beans his mother had thrown out of the window into the garden had sprung up into a big beanstalk which went up and up and up till it reached the sky. So the man spoke truth after all.

The beanstalk grew up quite close past Jack's window, so all he had to do was to open it and give a jump on to the beanstalk which ran up just like a big ladder. So Jack climbed, and he climbed and he climbed and he climbed and he climbed and he climbed and he climbed till at last he reached the sky. And when he got there he found a long broad road going as straight as a dart. So he walked along and he walked along and he walked along till he came to a great big tall house, and on the doorstep there was a great big tall woman.

'Good morning, mum,' says Jack, quite polite-like. 'Could you be so kind as to give me some breakfast?' For he hadn't had anything to eat, you know, the night before and was as hungry as a hunter.

'It's breakfast you want, is it?' says the great big tall woman, 'it's breakfast you'll be if you don't move off from here. My man is an ogre and there's nothing he likes better than boys broiled on toast. You'd better be moving on or he'll be coming.'

'Oh! please, mum, do give me something to eat, mum. I've had nothing to eat since yesterday morning, really and truly, mum,' says Jack. 'I may as well be broiled as die of hunger.'

Well, the ogre's wife was not half so bad after all. So she took Jack into the kitchen, and gave him a hunk of bread and cheese and a jug of milk. But Jack hadn't half finished these when thump! thump! thump! the whole house began to tremble with the noise of someone coming.

'Goodness gracious me! It's my old man,' said the ogre's wife, 'what on earth shall I do? Come along quick and jump in here.' And she bundled Jack into the oven just as the ogre came in.

He was a big one, to be sure. At his belt he had three calves strung up by the heels, and he unhooked them and threw them down on the table and said: 'Here, wife, broil me a couple of these for breakfast. Ah! what's this I smell?

'Fee-fi-fo-fum,
I smell the blood of an Englishman,
Be he alive or be he dead,
I'll have his bones to grind my bread.'

'Nonsense, dear,' said his wife, 'you're dreaming. Or perhaps you smell the scraps of that little boy you liked so much for yesterday's dinner. Here, you go and have a wash and tidy up, and by the time you come back your breakfast'll be ready for you.'

So off the ogre went, and Jack was just going to jump out of the oven and run away when the woman told him not. 'Wait till he's asleep,' says she; 'he always has a doze after breakfast.'

Well, the ogre had his breakfast, and after that he goes to a big chest and takes out of it a couple of bags of gold, and down he sits and counts till at last his head began to nod and he began to snore till the whole house shook again.

Then Jack crept out on tiptoe from his oven, and as he was passing the ogre he took one of the bags of gold under his arm, and off he pelters till he came to the beanstalk, and then he threw down the bag of gold, which, of course, fell into his mother's garden, and then he climbed down and climbed down till at last he got home and told his mother and showed her the gold and said: 'Well, mother, wasn't I right about the beans? They are really magical, you see.'

So they lived on the bag of gold for some time, but at last they came to the end of it, and Jack made up his mind to try his luck once more at the top of the beanstalk. So one fine morning he rose up early, and got on to the beanstalk, and he climbed and he climbed and he climbed and he climbed and he climbed and he climbed till at last he came out on to the road again and up to the great big tall house he had been to before. There, sure enough, was the great big tall woman a-standing on the doorstep.

'Good morning, mum,' says Jack, as bold as brass, 'could you be so good as to give me something to eat?'

'Go away, my boy,' said the big tall woman, 'or else my man will eat you up for breakfast. But aren't you the youngster who came here once before? Do you know, that very day my man missed one of his bags of gold.'

'That's strange, mum,' said Jack, 'I dare say I could tell you something about that, but I'm so hungry I can't speak till I've had something to eat.'

Well, the big tall woman was so curious that she took him in and gave him something to eat. But he had scarcely begun munching it as slowly as he could when thump! thump! they heard the giant's footstep, and his wife hid Jack away in the oven.

All happened as it did before. In came the ogre as he did before, said: 'Fee-fi-fo-fum,' and had his breakfast off three broiled oxen. Then he said: 'Wife, bring me the hen that lays the golden eggs.' So she brought it, and the ogre said: 'Lay,' and it laid an egg all of gold. And then the ogre began to nod his head, and to snore till the house shook.

Then Jack crept out of the oven on tiptoe, and caught hold of the golden hen, and was off before you could say 'Jack Robinson'. But this time the hen gave a cackle which woke the ogre, and just as Jack got out of the house he heard him calling: 'Wife, wife, what have you done with my golden hen?'

And the wife said: 'Why, my dear?'

But that was all Jack heard, for he rushed off to the beanstalk and climbed down like a house on fire. And when he got home he showed his mother the wonderful hen, and said 'Lay' to it; and it laid a golden egg every time he said 'Lay.'

Well, Jack was not content, and it wasn't long before he determined to have another try at his luck up there at the top of the beanstalk. So one fine morning, he rose up early, and got on to the beanstalk, and he climbed and he climbed and he climbed and he climbed till he got to the top. But this time he knew better than to go straight to the ogre's house. And when he got near it, he waited behind a bush till he saw the ogre's wife come out with a pail to get some water, and then he crept into the house and got into the copper. He hadn't been there long when he heard thump! thump! thump! as before, and in came the ogre and his wife.

'Fee-fi-fo-fum, I smell the blood of an Englishman,' cried out the ogre. 'I smell him, wife, I smell him.'

'Do you, my dearie?' says the ogre's wife. 'Then, if it's that little rogue that stole your gold and the hen that laid the golden eggs he's sure to have got into the oven.' And they both rushed to the oven. But Jack wasn't there, luckily, and the ogre's wife said: 'There you are again with your fee-fi-fo-fum. Why, of course, it's the boy you caught last night that I've just broiled for your breakfast. How forgetful I am, and how careless you are not to know the difference between live and dead after all these years.'

So the ogre sat down to the breakfast and ate it, but every now and then he would mutter: 'Well, I could have sworn – ' and he'd get up and search the larder and the cupboards and everything, only, luckily, he didn't think of the copper.

After breakfast was over, the ogre called out: 'Wife, wife, bring me my golden harp.' So she brought it and put it on the table before him. Then he said: 'Sing!' and the golden harp sang most beautifully. And it went on singing till the ogre fell asleep, and commenced to snore like thunder.

Then Jack lifted up the copper-lid very quietly and got down like a mouse and crept on hands and knees till he came to the table, when up he crawled, caught hold of the golden harp and dashed with it towards the door. But the harp called out quite loud: 'Master! Master!' and the ogre woke up just in time to see Jack running off with his harp.

Jack ran as fast as he could, and the ogre came rushing after, and would soon have caught him only Jack had a start and dodged him a bit and knew where he was going. When he got to the beanstalk the ogre was not much more than twenty yards away when suddenly he saw Jack disappear like, and when he came to the end of the road he saw Jack underneath climbing down for dear life. Well, the ogre didn't like trusting himself to such a ladder, and he stood and waited, so Jack got another start. But just then the harp cried out: 'Master! Master!' and the ogre swung himself down on to the beanstalk, which shook with his weight. Down climbs Jack, and after him climbed the ogre. By this time Jack had climbed down and climbed down and climbed down till he was very nearly home. So he called out: 'Mother! Mother! bring me an axe, bring me an axe.' And his mother came rushing out with the axe in her hand, but when she came to the beanstalk she stood stock still with fright, for there she saw the ogre with his legs just through the clouds.

But Jack jumped down and got hold of the axe and gave a chop at the beanstalk which cut it half in two. The ogre felt the beanstalk shake and quiver, so he stopped to see what was the matter. Then Jack gave another chop with the axe, and the beanstalk was cut in two and began to topple over. Then the ogre fell down and broke his crown, and the beanstalk came toppling after.

Then Jack showed his mother his golden harp, and what with showing that and selling the golden eggs, Jack and his mother became very rich, and he married a great princess, and they lived happy ever after.

Translator's note: This version of the story was written down by Joseph Jacobs in his 'English Fairy Tales' of 1890. But we can tell that it is much older than that. The famous verse beginning 'Fee-fi-fo-fum, I smell the blood of an Englishman' appears nearly three hundred years earlier: in his play 'King Lear', William Shakespeare gives the line to one of his characters, who is pretending to be mad and chants, 'His word was still Fie, foh, and fum, I smell the blood of a British man.'

British folk tradition has several stories called, as a group, 'Jack Tales', in which a country boy called Jack seems to be a fool, but turns out to be quick-witted, defeats giants and ogres, and takes their treasure. Such stories travel far and wide. Jacobs writes: 'I tell this as it was told me in Australia, somewhere about the year 1860.'

The Master Cat

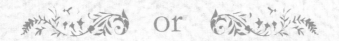 or

PUSS IN BOOTS

nce upon a time there was a miller who had nothing to leave his three children when he died but his mill, his donkey and his cat. They were soon shared out, and there was no need for the three young men to call in a notary and a lawyer, who would have eaten up their whole inheritance in no time at all. The eldest son got the mill, the second son had the donkey, and the youngest was left with nothing but the cat.

The youngest son was in despair when he thought of his hard fate. 'My brothers can earn an honest living if they work together,' he said, 'but when I've eaten my cat and made a muff of his fur, I shall die of starvation.'

The cat overheard this, but he didn't show it. Looking very sober and serious, he told the youngest son, 'Don't be so sad, master. All you have to do is give me a sack, have a pair of boots made for me so that I can walk through the countryside, and you'll soon see that you're better off than you thought.'

Although the young man didn't pin too much hope on these words, he had seen the cat catch rats and mice with such skill and agility, hanging from his paws or hiding in the flour playing dead, that he didn't give up hope. Puss might yet be able to help him in his hour of need.

When the cat had what he had asked for he put on the boots, slung the sack over his shoulder, took the strings that drew it shut in his forepaws, and went off to a warren where a great many rabbits lived. He put some bran and hogweed in his sack, lay down and

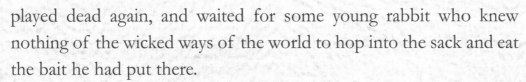

played dead again, and waited for some young rabbit who knew nothing of the wicked ways of the world to hop into the sack and eat the bait he had put there.

No sooner was he lying down than he got what he wanted. A silly young rabbit jumped into his sack, and the Master Cat, pulling the strings to close it, caught the rabbit and killed it without mercy.

Full of pride in his catch, he went to the king's palace and asked to speak to him. He was shown into His Majesty's chambers, where he made the king a low bow and said, 'Here, Sire, is a rabbit that the Marquis of Carabas has told me to bring you as a gift from him.' That was the name he had decided to give his master.

'Tell your master,' replied the king, 'that I thank him, and he has given me pleasure.'

Another time Puss hid in a wheat-field with his sack open, and when two partridges fluttered into it he pulled the strings and trapped them both. Then he took them to the king and made him a present of them, just as he had done with the rabbit. Once again the king was happy to receive the brace of partridges, and he had Puss offered something to drink.

So the cat went on like this for two or three months, bringing the king presents of game from his master from time to time. One day, when he knew that the king was going to walk on the banks of the river with his daughter, who was the most beautiful princess in the world, he told his master, 'Do as I say and your fortune is made! You have only to bathe in the river at a place that I'll show you. Leave the rest to me.'

The Marquis of Carabas did as his cat told him, though he couldn't see what good would come of it. As he was bathing in the river the king passed by, and the cat began shouting with all his might, 'Help, help! The Marquis of Carabas is drowning!'

Hearing these cries, the king put his head out of the carriage window, and when he recognised the cat who had so often brought him game, he told his guards to make haste to help the Marquis of Carabas.

As they were pulling the poor marquis out of the river, the cat went up to the carriage and told the king that thieves had stolen his master's clothes while he was bathing, in spite of his loud cries of 'Stop thief!' But the clever cat himself had really hidden them under a large rock.

The king immediately told his chamberlains to go and find one of his best suits for the Marquis of Carabas, and showed him many marks of favour. Since the fine clothes that were brought for the marquis set off his looks to good advantage (for he was a handsome, well-built young man), the king's daughter took a great liking to him, and by the time the Marquis of Carabas had cast her two or three very respectful and rather affectionate glances she had fallen madly in love with him.

The king asked the marquis to get into the carriage and join him and the princess on their drive. Delighted to see that his plans were beginning to work, the cat went ahead of them, and when he met some peasants mowing a meadow he told them, 'Good mowers, if you don't tell the king that the meadow you're mowing belongs to the

Marquis of Carabas, you'll all be made into mincemeat.'

Sure enough, the king asked the mowers who owned the meadow that they were mowing.

'Oh,' they all said in chorus, 'it belongs to the Marquis of Carabas.' For the cat's threat had terrified them.

'You have a fine meadow here,' said the king to the Marquis of Carabas.

'As you see, Your Majesty,' replied the marquis, 'it gives a good crop of hay every year.'

The Master Cat, still running on ahead, met some people reaping wheat, and told them, 'Good reapers, if you don't say that these wheat-fields belong to the Marquis of Carabas, you'll all be made into mincemeat.'

The king passed by a moment later, and asked who owned all the wheat-fields that he saw.

'Oh, the Marquis of Carabas,' replied the reapers, and the king congratulated the marquis.

The cat, still going ahead of the carriage all the time, kept saying the same to all the peasants he met, and the king was amazed to see what great estates the Marquis of Carabas possessed.

At last the Master Cat came to a fine castle. It belonged to an ogre, the richest ever known, and all the land through which the king had driven really belonged to this castle. After finding out who the ogre was and what he could do, the cat asked to speak to him, saying that he didn't want to pass so close to his castle without paying his humble respects.

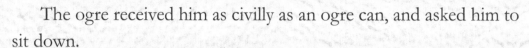

The ogre received him as civilly as an ogre can, and asked him to sit down.

'I've been told,' said the cat, 'that you can change yourself into all kinds of animals. For instance, people say you can turn into a lion or an elephant.'

'That's true,' replied the ogre, 'and just to show you, watch me turn into a lion!'

The cat was so frightened when he saw a lion in front of him that he immediately scampered up to the castle gutters, not without danger and difficulty, because his boots weren't made for walking on the rooftops.

After a while, seeing that the ogre had returned to his real shape, the cat came down and admitted that he had been afraid.

'And I've even been told,' said the cat, 'although I really can't believe it, that you can turn into the smallest of animals too, such as a rat or a mouse, although I must confess I think that's completely impossible.'

'Impossible?' said the ogre. 'Just watch this!'

And so saying, he turned into a mouse which began scurrying about the floor. No sooner did the cat see the mouse than he pounced on it and ate it up.

Meanwhile the king, seeing the ogre's fine castle as he passed by, decided to go in. On hearing the sound of the carriage driving over the drawbridge, the cat came out and said to the king, 'Welcome, Your Majesty, to the castle of my master the Marquis of Carabas!'

'What,' cried the king, 'is this castle yours too, Marquis? I never set eyes on anything finer than this courtyard and all the buildings around it. Do let us see inside, if you please!'

The marquis gave his hand to the young princess, and following the king, who went up the steps first, they entered a great hall where they found a magnificent feast ready. The ogre had ordered it for friends who were coming to see him that very day, but they dared not go in when they saw that the king was there. The king was delighted by the Marquis of Carabas, and so was his daughter, who was deeply in love with the young man. Seeing what great lands and possessions he owned, the king drank five or six glasses of wine, and then told him, 'Well, Marquis, if you'd care to be my son-in-law it's entirely up to you.'

The marquis, bowing very low, accepted the honour the king was doing him, and he married the princess that very day. As for the cat, he became a great lord, and never chased mice again except for fun.

Translator's note: *'Puss in Boots' is one of two stories in this book by Charles Perrault, whose 'Tales of Past Times' were first published in 1697. He wanted to bring the old country stories up to date and add a moral to the magic of their ogres and fairies. One of many stories in which a clever animal helps the hero to make his fortune, 'Puss in Boots' is now known mainly from Perrault's version.*

The Sea Rabbit

Once upon a time there was a princess who had a hall with twelve windows in her castle. It was high up under the battlements, and its windows looked out north, south, east and west, so that if she climbed up there and looked all around she had a view of her whole kingdom. She saw more keenly than other people out of the first window, she saw even better out of the second, she saw yet more clearly out of the third, and so on until the twelfth. Out of that one she saw all that was above and below the earth, and nothing could be hidden from her. But because she was proud, would bow to no one, and wanted to rule by herself, she let it be known that no one was to be her husband unless he could hide from her so well that she could never find him. And if anyone tried and she did find him, his head would be cut off and stuck on a stake.

There were ninety-seven stakes with dead heads on them round the castle by now, and it was a long time since any man had tried hiding from her. The princess was pleased, and she thought: now I shall be free all my life. Then three brothers came along, saying that they wanted to try their luck. The eldest thought he would be well hidden when he crept into a lime-pit, but she saw him from the very first window, and had him hauled out and his head cut off. The second crept into the castle cellar, but she saw him from the first window too, and that was the end of him: his head was stuck on the ninety-ninth stake. Then the youngest brother came to her and asked her to give him a day to think of his plan, and indeed to be gracious enough to give him another attempt if she found him. But if he failed three times, he said, he wouldn't want to live any longer. He was so handsome and asked with so much feeling that she said, 'Yes, I will grant your wishes, but you won't succeed.'

Next day he thought for a long time, wondering where to hide, but in vain. So he picked up his gun and went hunting. He saw a raven, and took aim at it. He was about to pull the trigger when the raven cried out, 'Don't shoot, and I will make it worth your while!' So he lowered his gun, went on, and came to a lake where he surprised a large fish which had come up from below to the surface of the water. When he had it in his sights, the fish cried, 'Don't shoot, and I will make it worth your while!' He let the fish dive down again, went on, and met a limping fox. He shot at the fox and missed it, but the fox cried out, 'Come here and pull the thorn out of my foot!' He did as he was asked, but then he planned to kill and skin the fox. However, the fox said, 'Don't do it, and I will make it worth your while!' So the young man let him go, and as it was evening by now he went home.

Next day was the day when he was to hide, but however hard he racked his brains, he couldn't think where. He went into the forest to find the raven and said, 'I let you live, now tell me where to hide so that the princess can't see me.' The raven bowed its head and thought for a long time. At last it croaked, 'I know what!' It fetched an egg from its nest, broke it in two, and put the young man inside the shell; then it made the egg whole again and sat on it. When the princess went to the first window she couldn't see the young man, nor could she see him from the next window, and she began to feel afraid, but when she reached the eleventh window she saw him. She had the raven shot, the egg was brought to her and broken, and the young man had to come out. 'You have another chance,' she said, 'but if you don't do any better this time it'll be the end of you.'

Next day he went down to the lake, called the fish, and said, 'I let you live, now tell me where to hide so that the princess won't see me.'

The fish thought, and at last it said, 'I know what! I'll keep you hidden in my belly.' So it swallowed the young man and dived down to the bed of the lake. The princess looked through her windows and couldn't see him, even from the eleventh, and she was dismayed, but when she came to the twelfth window she saw him at last. She had the fish caught and killed, and the young man came out. You can imagine how he felt.

'You've had two chances,' said the princess. 'I think your head will end up on the hundredth stake.'

On the last day he went out into the fields, heavy at heart, and there he met the fox. 'You know so many hiding-places,' he said. 'I let you live, now tell me a place to hide where the princess won't find me.'

'That won't be easy,' said the fox, looking thoughtful. At last it cried, 'I know what!' And it took the young man to a spring, jumped into the water, and came out in the shape of a market pedlar and animal-dealer. The young man had to plunge into the water too, and he came out in the shape of a little sea rabbit.

The pedlar went to town and showed the pretty little animal. A great many people gathered to look at it. Last of all the princess came along, and since she liked the sea rabbit she bought it and gave the

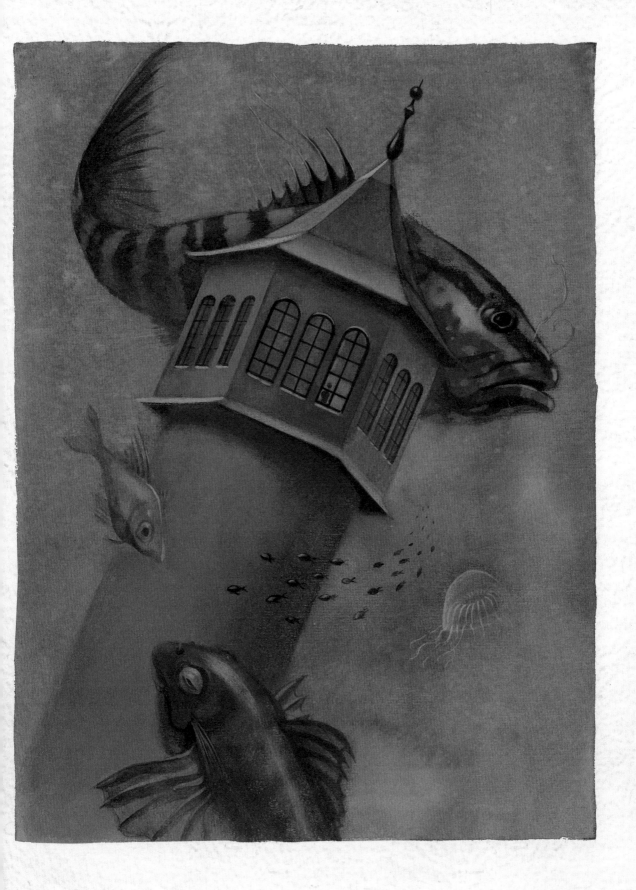

pedlar a great deal of money in return. Before he gave it to her, the fox told the sea rabbit, 'When the princess goes to her window, you must be quick and creep under her braided hair.'

Now the time came when she was to look for the young man. She went to her windows from the first to the eleventh in turn, and she didn't see him. When she couldn't see him from the twelfth window either she was full of fear and rage, and struck the pane so hard that the glass in all the windows broke into a thousand pieces and the whole castle trembled.

She stepped back, and feeling the sea rabbit under her braid she seized it, flung it to the floor, and cried, 'Go away, get out of my sight!' It ran to the pedlar, and the two of them hurried to the spring, where they plunged into the water and returned to their true forms. The young man thanked the fox, and said, 'The raven and the fish were simpletons compared to you. You know all the right tricks, and that's a fact!'

Now the young man went straight back to the castle. The princess was waiting for him, resigned to her fate. Their wedding was held, and now he was king and lord of the whole kingdom. He never told her where he had hidden the third time, or who had helped him, so she believed he had done it all through his own skill, and she respected him, saying to herself, he knows more than you do!

Translator's note: The German for a guinea pig literally means 'little sea pig', and the curious 'sea rabbit' in this story is a word formed in the same way. The tale contains the themes of a 'perilous bride' – a girl who doesn't want to be married and threatens her unsuccessful suitors with death – and several helpful animals. The fox is always regarded as particularly cunning in folklore.

The Iron Stove

In the old days, when wishes still came true, an old witch cast a spell on a prince and made him sit in the forest inside a big iron stove. He spent many years there, and no one could break the spell. One day a princess came into the forest. She was lost, and couldn't find her way back to her father's kingdom. After nine days of wandering around, she finally found herself in front of the iron stove. Then a voice came out of it and asked, 'Where do you come from, and where are you going?'

'I've lost my way to my father's kingdom,' she said, 'and now I can't go home again.'

'I'll help you to get home,' said the voice in the iron stove, 'and soon too, if you'll sign an agreement to do as I ask. I am the son of a greater king than your father, and I want to marry you.'

She was frightened, and thought: dear God, whatever will I do, married to an iron stove? But she wanted to get home to her father so much that she said she would do as the stove asked, and signed the agreement.

Then the stove said, 'You must come back with a knife and scrape a hole in the iron.' And it gave her a companion to walk beside her. Her companion said never a word, but brought her home again in just two hours.

Well, there were great rejoicings in the castle when the princess came back, and the old king flung his arms around her and kissed her. But she was very sad. 'Dear Father, you don't know what's happened to me!' she said. 'I'd never have found my way home out of the great wild forest if I hadn't come upon an iron stove, but in exchange I had to sign an agreement to go back into the forest, break the spell on it and marry it.'

That alarmed the old king so much that he nearly fainted away, for he had only this one daughter. So it was decided that instead of the princess they would send the miller's daughter, who was very beautiful. They took the girl out to the forest, gave her a knife, and told her to scrape a hole in the iron stove. She scraped away for twenty-four hours, but she couldn't even scratch the stove.

As dawn came, the voice in the stove said, 'I think it's day outside.'

'I think so too,' the girl replied. 'I think I hear the clatter of my father's mill.'

'Oh, you're a miller's daughter, are you? Go home and send the princess here.'

So she went back and told the old king that the iron stove in the forest didn't want her, it wanted his daughter.

The king was dismayed, and his daughter wept. But there was still the swineherd's daughter, who was even more beautiful than the miller's daughter, and they planned to give her some money to go out to the iron stove instead of the princess. So she was taken into the forest, and had to scrape away at the stove for twenty-four hours, but she couldn't even scratch it.

When dawn came, the voice in the stove said, 'I think it's day outside.'

'I think so too,' she replied. 'I think I hear my father blowing his horn.'

'Oh, you're a swineherd's daughter, are you? Go home again and send the princess here. Tell her it will all be just as I promised, but if she doesn't come everything in her father's kingdom will fall into ruin, and there won't be one stone left standing on another.'

When the princess heard that she began to weep, but there was nothing for it, she would have to keep her promise. So she said goodbye to her father, took a knife, and went out to the iron stove in the forest. When she got there she began to scrape, the iron yielded to the knife, and after two hours she had scraped a small hole. She looked through it, and saw such a handsome young man, all glittering with gold and jewels, that she fell in love with him at once. So she went on scraping, and made the hole large enough for him to come out. Then he said, 'You are mine and I am yours, you have broken the spell and you're my promised bride.'

He was going to take her to his own kingdom, but she asked to be allowed to go and see her father once again, and the prince agreed, but she must speak no more than three words to her father, he said, and she was to come straight back. So she went home, but she spoke more than three words, and then the iron stove immediately disappeared and was taken far away, over glass mountains and across sharp swords, but the spell on the prince had been broken and he wasn't inside it any more. After that she said goodbye to her father, took a little money with her but not much, and went back into the great forest looking for the iron stove. However, it was nowhere to be found.

She spent nine days looking for it, and then she was so hungry

that she didn't know what to do, for she had nothing left to eat. When evening came, she climbed a small tree and thought of spending the night up there, because she was afraid of the wild animals in the forest. At midnight, however, she saw a little light far away, and thought, oh, I'll be safe there! So she climbed out of the tree and set off towards the little light, praying as she walked along. Then she came to a little old cottage with grass growing round it, and a little woodpile in front of the door. Oh, she thought, whatever is this place? Looking through the window, she saw nothing inside but toads both large and small, and a table well laid with wine and roast meat, and the plates and goblets were silver. So she plucked up her courage and knocked. A fat toad immediately cried:

'Little lady green,
Say, what's to be seen?
Hop along on brownie feet
Hop along fast and fleet.
Open the door wide
Let's see who's outside.'

Then a small toad came hopping up and opened the door to the princess. When she came in all the toads welcomed her and made her sit down. 'Where do you come from, and where are you going?' they asked. So she told them everything that had happened to her, and how the iron stove and the prince had disappeared, because she had broken her promise not to speak more than three words. Now, she said, she was going to wander over mountains and through valleys, searching until she found him.

At that the fat old toad said:

'Little lady green
What more's to be seen?
Hop along on brownie feet
Hop along fast and fleet.
Hop along and see
You bring the box to me.'

So the little toad went and brought her a big box. After that they gave the princess food and drink, and took her to a nicely made bed as soft as silk and velvet, where she lay down and fell asleep in God's name. Next morning she got up, and the old toad gave her three needles out of the big box and said she must take them with her. She would need them, said the toad, for she would have to climb a high glass mountain and cross three sharp swords and a wide water. If she did all that, then she would get her beloved prince back again. The toad gave her three things which she was to keep most carefully: the three needles, a plough-wheel, and three nuts.

She went away with those things, and when she came to the

smooth glass mountain she stuck the three needles in it, first behind her feet and then in front of them again, and so she climbed over it, and when she was across she left the needles in a place that she was sure to remember. After that she came to the three sharp swords. She stood on her plough-wheel and rolled over them. At last she came to the wide water, and when she had crossed it she saw a fine, large castle. She went in and asked for work, saying that she was a poor servant girl and would be glad to hire herself out. But all the time she knew that the prince she had saved from the iron stove in the great forest was in there. So she was taken on as a kitchen-maid for very low wages.

Now the prince had another girl at his side and was going to marry her, for he thought the princess had died long ago. In the evening, when she had finished washing the dishes, she felt in her pocket and found the three nuts that the old toad had given her. She bit one open, thinking she would eat the kernel, but lo and behold,

there was a fine, royal dress inside it instead. When the prince's bride heard about it, she came to look at the dress and wanted to buy it, saying it was no dress for a serving-maid. Then the princess said no, she didn't want to sell it, but if the bride would grant her one thing, to let her sleep a night in the bridegroom's room, she should have it. The bride agreed, because the dress was so beautiful and she had nothing so fine. As it was evening, she told her bridegroom, 'The silly girl wants to sleep in your room.'

'If you don't mind, then neither do I,' he said.

But she gave him a glass of wine into which she had put a sleeping draught. So the prince and the princess both went to sleep in his room, and he slept so soundly that she couldn't wake him. She wept all night, crying, 'I saved you from the wild forest and the iron stove, I've searched for you far and wide, I've climbed a glass mountain, I have crossed three sharp swords and the wide water to find you, and won't you hear me now?'

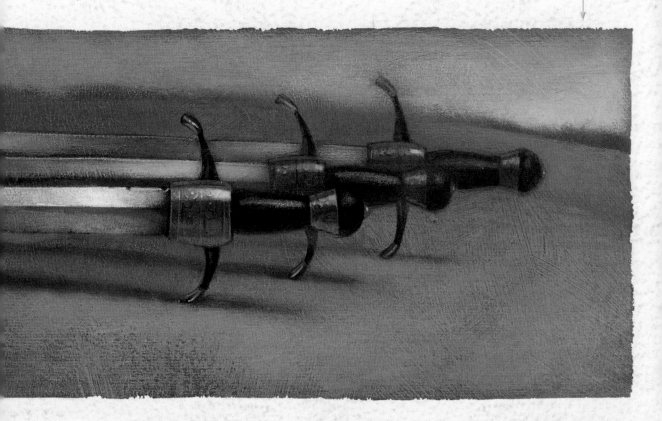

The servants sitting outside the door heard her weep all night like this, and in the morning they told their master. So next evening, when she had washed the dishes, she bit the second nut open, and there was an even more beautiful dress inside it. When the bride saw it she wanted to buy this dress too. But the girl would take no money for it, and asked instead to spend another night in the bridegroom's bedroom. However, the bride gave him another sleeping draught, and he slept so soundly that he could hear nothing. As for the kitchen-maid, she wept all night, crying, 'I saved you from the wild forest and the iron stove, I've searched for you far and wide, I've climbed a glass mountain, I have crossed three sharp swords and the wide water to find you, and won't you hear me now?'

Once again the servants sitting outside the door heard her weep all night like this, and in the morning they told their master. And on the third evening, when she had washed the dishes, she bit the third nut open and found a yet more beautiful dress inside it, stiff with pure gold. When the bride saw it, she wanted to have it, but the girl would give it to her only if she could spend a third night in the bridegroom's bedroom. This time, the prince took care to pour the sleeping draught away. When she began weeping and crying, 'My dearest one, I saved you from the wild forest and the iron stove,' the prince leaped up and said, 'You are my true bride, you are mine and I am yours.'

That very night he set out with her in a carriage, and they took away the false bride's clothes so that she couldn't get up. When they came to the wide water they took a ferry over it, and when they came to the three sharp swords they stood on the plough-wheel, and when they came to the glass mountain they stuck the three needles into it. So at last they came to the little old cottage, but when they went in it was a great castle; the spell on all the toads had been broken, and they were princes and princesses, all rejoicing. Then the wedding was held, and the prince and his bride stayed in the castle, which was much bigger than her father's. But because the old man was sad to think of being left alone, they drove off and brought him to live with them. So now they had two kingdoms, and they lived happily ever after.

There's a mouse in the clover
My story is over.

Translator's note: Certain episodes or 'themes' often turn up in more than one fairy tale. 'The Iron Stove' is one of two stories in this book featuring a glass mountain that must be climbed, with magical aid, by the hero or, as here, the heroine. This very common theme is also found in British traditional stories: a particularly fine Scottish story is 'The Black Bull of Norroway'. These 'glass mountain' stories are good examples of tales where an active, resourceful heroine is the central figure.

Cinderella

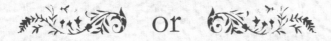 or

THE LITTLE
GLASS SLIPPER

There was once a gentleman whose second wife was the proudest and haughtiest woman ever seen. She had two daughters just like her in every way. As for her new husband, he too had a daughter of his own, but she was as kind and gentle as anyone could wish. She inherited her disposition from her mother, who had been the best woman in the world.

As soon as the wedding was over the girl's stepmother showed how bad-tempered she was. She couldn't bear her stepdaughter's good, kind nature, because it showed how bad her own daughters were. She gave her the hardest work around the house to do. The girl washed the dishes and scoured the steps, cleaned milady's chamber and her fine daughters' bedrooms. She herself slept in the attic on a wretched straw mattress, while her sisters had rooms with polished wooden floors and the most fashionable beds, and mirrors where they could see themselves from head to toe.

The poor girl patiently put up with all these trials, and dared not complain to her father, who was entirely under his wife's thumb and would only have scolded her.

When she had finished her work, she used to go and sit among the cinders in the chimney corner, so the rest of the household generally called her 'Cinder-squatter'. But the younger of her two stepsisters, who wasn't quite as spiteful as the elder girl, called her Cinderella. In spite of her shabby clothes, Cinderella was a hundred times prettier than her sisters in their magnificent gowns.

Now it so happened that the king's son was going to give a ball, and he invited everyone of high rank. Our two fine young ladies were to be among the guests, because they cut a very grand figure in society. So they were very pleased, and set about choosing the gowns and head-dresses that would suit them best. That meant even more work for Cinderella, since she had to iron her sisters' underclothes and starch their cuffs. They talked of nothing but the clothes they were going to wear to the ball.

'I shall go in my red velvet dress with the English trimming,' said the older sister.

'I shall wear my ordinary skirt,' said the younger sister, 'but to make up for that I'll put on my coat with the gold-flowered embroidery and my diamond brooch, which is something quite out of the ordinary.'

They sent for a good milliner to make them elaborate caps, and they bought the best beauty spots available. They called in Cinderella to ask her opinion, because she had good taste. Cinderella gave them excellent advice, and even said she would do their hair for them, an offer that they were very ready to accept.

As she was doing their hair, they asked her, 'Wouldn't you like to go to the ball too, Cinderella?'

'Oh, sisters, you're making fun of me,' she said. 'It's not my place to go.'

'You're quite right – how everyone would laugh to see a Cinder-squatter at the ball!'

Anyone but Cinderella would have done their hair badly after that, but she was as good as good can be and took particular care with it. In their transports of delight they had eaten nothing for nearly two days. More than a dozen stay-laces were broken as they tried to squeeze themselves into corsets to make their waists look smaller, and they spent all their time in front of the mirror.

At last the happy day came, and when her sisters left Cinderella watched them go until they were out of sight. Then she began to weep.

Her godmother, seeing her in floods of tears, asked what the matter was.

'Oh,' said Cinderella, 'I would like – I would so like …' But she was crying so hard that she couldn't finish what she was saying.

Her godmother, who was a fairy, said, 'You'd like to go to the ball, wouldn't you?'

'Oh yes, I would,' said Cinderella, sighing.

'Well, be a good girl,' said her godmother, 'and I'll make sure that you do.' She took her to her room and said, 'Go out into the garden and fetch me a pumpkin.'

Cinderella immediately went to pick the best pumpkin she could find and took it to her godmother, though she couldn't think how a pumpkin would help her to go to the ball.

Her godmother hollowed it out, and when there was nothing left but the rind she touched it with her magic wand, and at once the pumpkin was turned into a beautiful golden coach.

Then she went to look in the mousetrap, where she found six live mice. She told Cinderella to open the catch of the trap a little way, and as each mouse came out she tapped it with her wand. The mice immediately turned into handsome horses, a fine team of six with mouse-coloured coats of dapple grey.

As her godmother was wondering what she could turn into a coachman, Cinderella said, 'I'll go and see if there's a rat in the rat trap to make a coachman for us.'

'That's a good idea,' said her godmother. 'Go and look.' So Cinderella brought her the rat trap, and there were three fat rats inside. The fairy chose one of the three because of his handsome whiskers, and when she had touched him with her wand he was changed into a stout coachman with one of the finest moustaches ever seen.

Next she told Cinderella, 'Go into the garden, and you'll find six lizards behind the watering can. Bring them here to me.'

No sooner had she brought the lizards than her godmother turned them into six footmen who immediately got up behind the carriage in their braided liveries, and clung on as if they had never done anything else in their lives.

'There,' said the fairy to Cinderella, 'now you have a coach to take you to the ball! Aren't you pleased?'

'Oh yes, but how can I go like this, in my shabby clothes?'

Her godmother just touched her with the magic wand, and her clothes were immediately changed into a dress made of cloth of gold and silver, and embroidered with precious stones. Next she gave her the prettiest little pair of glass slippers in the world.

When Cinderella was dressed in these fine things she got into the coach, and her godmother told her that whatever happened she mustn't stay at the ball beyond midnight. If she was there a moment longer, said the fairy, her coach would turn back into a pumpkin, her horses into mice, her footmen into lizards, and she would be wearing her old clothes again.

Cinderella promised her godmother that she would be sure to leave the ball before the stroke of twelve, and off she went, with her heart full of joy.

When the king's son was told that a great princess had just arrived, but no one knew who she was, he made haste to welcome her. He gave her his hand to help her out of the coach, and led her into the ballroom where the company was all assembled.

There was complete silence; the guests stopped dancing and the musicians stopped playing as everyone admired the unknown beauty. All that could be heard was a soft murmur of, 'Oh, how lovely she is!'

The king himself, old as he was, couldn't take his eyes off her, and told the queen in a low voice that it was a long time since he had seen such a beautiful, charming young woman. All the ladies took careful notice of her hairstyle and every detail of her gown, so that they could get one just the same made next day, always supposing they could find dress material and dressmakers good enough. The prince showed her to a seat of honour, and then asked her to open the next dance with him. She danced with such grace that the guests admired her even more.

Delicious refreshments were served, but the prince couldn't eat a morsel, he was so busy looking at her. She went to sit down with her sisters, said a great many kind things, and offered them some of the oranges and lemons that the prince had given her. They were very much surprised, for they didn't recognise her at all.

While they were talking, Cinderella heard the clock strike a quarter to twelve. At that, she made a deep curtsey to the company and went away as fast as she could. As soon as she was home she went to find her godmother, and after thanking her said how much she would like to go to the ball again next day, because the prince had invited her.

While she was telling her godmother everything that had happened at the ball, the two sisters knocked at the door and Cinderella went to open it.

'How late you are coming home!' she told them, yawning, rubbing her eyes and stretching as if she had only just woken up. However, she hadn't felt in the least sleepy since the three of them parted.

'Oh, if only you'd been to the ball,' one of her sisters said, 'you certainly wouldn't have been bored. The most beautiful princess ever seen was there, and she was so kind and attentive to us, and gave us some oranges and lemons.'

Cinderella was overjoyed, and asked the princess's name, but they told her that no one knew, and the prince was in great distress and would give anything in the world to find out who she was.

Cinderella smiled, and told them, 'Well, she must indeed have been beautiful! Oh, how lucky you are! Couldn't I see her too? Miss Javotte, do please lend me your yellow dress, the one you wear every day.'

'Well, really, what an idea!' said Miss Javotte. 'Lend my dress to an ugly Cinder-squatter like you? I'd have to be out of my mind!'

Cinderella was expecting a refusal, and was glad, for she would have been in an awkward fix if her sister had agreed to lend her dress.

Next day the two sisters went to the ball again, and so did Cinderella, in an even finer gown than the evening before. The prince stayed close to her and kept paying her compliments. She was not in the least bored, and so she forgot her godmother's good advice and heard the first stroke of midnight when she had thought it wasn't even eleven yet. She leaped up and ran away, as swift and light on her feet as a deer.

The prince followed, but he couldn't catch up with her. However, she had left one of her little glass slippers behind, and he picked it up with great care.

Cinderella arrived home out of breath, without her coach and footmen and in her shabby old clothes. Nothing was left of all her magnificence except one of her little slippers, the partner to the one she had left behind.

The guards at the palace gates were asked if they had seen a princess leaving, but they said they had seen only a girl in very shabby clothes, who looked more like a peasant than a lady of quality.

When the two sisters came back from the ball Cinderella asked if they had enjoyed it again, and if the beautiful lady had been there. They said yes, but she had run away on the stroke of midnight, in such a hurry that she left one of her little glass slippers behind. It was the prettiest slipper in the world. The prince had picked it up and did nothing but gaze at it for the rest of the ball. He was certainly deeply in love with the beautiful lady to whom the little slipper belonged, they said.

They were telling the truth, for only a few days later the king's son had a proclamation read out, to the sound of trumpets, saying that he would marry the lady whose foot the slipper fitted perfectly. First the princesses tried it on, then the duchesses, and then the rest of the court ladies, but it was no use.

The slipper was brought to the two sisters' house, and they did all they could to squeeze their feet into the slipper, but they couldn't do it. Cinderella, watching them and recognising her slipper, smiled and said, 'Let me see if I can get it on!'

Her sisters began laughing and making fun of her. But the gentleman who was taking the slipper round to try it on ladies looked closely at Cinderella and saw how pretty she was. He said that was only right, and he had orders to let all young women try on the slipper, so he made Cinderella sit down, and when he raised the slipper to her little foot he saw that it fitted as perfectly as if it had been made of wax.

The two sisters were astonished, and they were even more surprised when Cinderella took the other little slipper out of her pocket and put it on. And now her godmother arrived, touched Cinderella's clothes with her magic wand and made them even more magnificent than the ball dresses she had worn before.

Now her two sisters recognised her as the beautiful princess they had seen at the ball. They threw themselves at her feet, begging her to forgive them for all their unkind treatment of her. Cinderella raised them from the ground, kissed them and said she forgave them with all her heart, and she hoped they would love her always.

Then she was taken to the young prince in her fine clothes. He thought she looked more beautiful than ever, and a few days later he married her. Cinderella, who was as good as she was beautiful, gave her two sisters apartments in the palace, and married them that same day to two noblemen of the court.

Translator's note: We know the story of 'Cinderella' best from this version by Perrault. The famous glass slipper was probably not really meant to be glass at all; people think that Perrault misheard the word vair (fur) as verre (glass), which sounds just the same in French. There are very many other versions of the story. In some of them the heroine plays a more active part than in Perrault's version, but she is always persecuted by her step-family and has some magical person or animal to help her to win the prince's hand, in this case her fairy godmother.

The Bremen Town Band

There was once a man who had a donkey, and the donkey had carried sacks to the mill for many long years, never tiring. However, his strength was failing him, and he was less and less use for work. So his master was thinking of getting rid of him. Guessing what was in the air, the donkey ran away and set out for Bremen, where he thought he could join the town band as a musician.

When he had been going along for a while he met a dog lying in the road, breathing heavily as if he had been running until he was worn out. 'Why are you panting like that, Grabber?' asked the donkey.

'Oh dear,' said the dog, 'because I'm old, and getting weaker every day. I'm no use for hunting any more, so my master was going to kill me. I ran away, but how can I earn a living now?'

'I tell you what,' said the donkey. 'I'm on my way to Bremen to join the town band. Why don't you come with me and be a musician too? I'll play the lute and you can beat the drums.'

The dog liked the sound of that, so they went along together.

Before long they met a cat sitting in the road, looking as dismal as three days of wet weather. 'Well, what's the matter with you, old Whiskers?' asked the donkey.

'It's no joke when people want to kill you,' said the cat. 'Now that I'm growing old, my teeth are getting blunt, and I'd rather sit behind the stove and purr than hunt mice, so my mistress tried to drown me. I made my escape, but now I don't know what to do. Where am I to go?'

'Come to Bremen with us,' said the donkey. 'You're used to singing serenades, so you can be a town musician there.'

The cat thought that was a good idea, and he went with them. On the road the three runaways passed a farm where a rooster was sitting on the gate, crowing for all he was worth.

'You're crowing fit to wake the dead,' said the donkey. 'What's the idea?'

'I was forecasting good weather,' said the rooster, 'because it's Our Lady's Day, when Mary has washed Baby Jesus's little shirts and wants to dry them. But because tomorrow is Sunday, and guests are coming, the farmer's cruel wife has told the cook to make me into chicken broth, so I'm to have my head cut off this evening. Now I'm crowing my heart out while I still can.'

'I tell you what, Redcrest,' said the donkey, 'why not come along with us? We're on our way to Bremen, and you're bound to find something better than death anywhere. You have a good strong voice, and if we all make music together we're sure to do all right.'

However, they couldn't reach the town of Bremen within the day, and that evening they came to a forest where they decided to spend the night. The donkey and the dog lay down under a large tree, the cat and the rooster climbed into its branches, and then the rooster flew right up to the top of the tree, which was the safest place for him. Before he went to sleep he looked in all directions again, and he thought he saw a little spark in the distance. He called down to his friends that there must be a house not far off, because he could see a light shining.

'Then let's set off for that house,' said the donkey. 'It's not very comfortable here.' And the dog thought he could do with a couple of bones that had a little meat left on them.

So they set off towards the place where the light was, and soon they saw it shining more clearly, and it grew larger and larger until they came to a robbers' house, all brightly lit up. The donkey, being the largest of them, went over to the window and looked in.

'What do you see, Greycoat?' asked the rooster.

'What do I see?' said the donkey. 'A table laid with good things to eat and drink, and robbers sitting there tucking into it all.'

'We could do with some of that,' said the rooster.

'Hee-haw, yes, I wish we were there!' said the donkey.

Then the animals tried to work out some way of chasing the robbers out of the house, and in the end they thought of one. The donkey put his fore-legs up on the window-sill, the dog jumped on the donkey's back, the cat climbed up on the dog, and last of all the rooster flew up and perched on the cat's head. When they were all in place and someone gave the word, they all began making music at once: the donkey brayed, the dog barked, the cat mewed and the rooster crowed. Then they charged through the window into the room with a great crash of breaking glass. The robbers leaped to their feet when they heard that fearsome noise, thinking that a ghost was coming in, and they ran away into the forest, terrified. Now the four friends sat down at the table, helped themselves to everything that was left, and ate as if they weren't going to eat again for the next four weeks.

When the four musicians had finished they put out the light and went to find somewhere to sleep, each according to his nature and where he felt most comfortable. The donkey lay down on the dungheap, the dog lay behind the door, the cat settled down on the stove among the warm ashes, and the rooster perched on the top rafter in the roof. They were tired after their long journey, so they soon fell asleep.

After midnight, when the robbers saw from a distance that there was no light in the house any more and everything seemed quiet, the robber captain said, 'We ought not to have run away in fright like that.' And he told one of his men to go back and search the house. The robber found it quiet, went into the kitchen for a light, and thinking that the cat's glowing, fiery eyes were live coals he held a sulphur match to them to set fire to it. But the cat wasn't having any of that, and leaped at his face, spitting and scratching. Terrified, he ran to escape through the back door, but the dog lying there jumped up and bit his leg. As he was running over the yard and past the dungheap, the donkey gave him a mighty kick with his back leg. And the rooster, roused by all this noise and wide awake now, called down from the rafter, 'Cock-a-doodle-do!'

The robber ran back to his captain as fast as his legs would carry him, crying, 'There's a dreadful witch in the house. She hissed at me and scratched my face with her long fingers. And in the doorway there's a man with a knife who stabbed me in the leg, and a big black monster who hit me with a wooden cudgel is lying in the yard, and up in the roof sits the judge shouting, "Bring that villain into court!" So I made my getaway.'

From then on the robbers dared not go back to their house, but the four town musicians of Bremen liked it there so much that they never left again. And the last man to tell this tale isn't dead yet.

***Translator's note:** This is one of the stories that Dorothea Viehmann, the tailor's widow, told the Grimm brothers, and we can easily imagine her hearing it told at her father's inn when she was a girl. Nothing actually magical happens in this humorous tale – unless of course we count the idea of animals being able to talk to each other. It is known all over the world in different versions, for instance from both Asia and Eastern Europe. Sometimes the robbers defeated by the animal musicians are a pack of wolves. The Grimms' version is particularly satisfying because of the resourceful way the animals, threatened with slaughter by ungrateful humans as they grow old, join together to improve their own lives and get the better of the cowardly robbers in the comic climax.*

The Girl with
No Hands

There was once a miller who had fallen on hard times, and had nothing left but his mill and a large apple tree that stood behind it. One day he had gone into the forest for firewood when an old man he had never seen before came up to him, and said, 'Why do you go to all that trouble chopping wood? Promise to give me what stands behind your mill, and I'll make you rich.'

Well, the miller thought to himself, what can that be but my apple tree? So he said yes, and signed it over to the stranger. The man laughed a mocking laugh and said, 'Then I'll come for my property in three years' time.' And away he went.

When the miller got home his wife came to meet him. 'Tell me, miller,' she said, 'where does this sudden wealth of ours come from? All our coffers are full. No one carried it all in, and I have no idea what's happened.'

He replied, 'It comes from a stranger who met me in the forest and promised me great riches. In return, I signed over what stands behind the mill to him. We can spare the old apple tree in exchange for such treasures, I'm sure.'

'Oh, husband,' said his wife, horrified. 'It was the Devil you met. He didn't mean the apple tree, he meant our daughter, who was standing behind the mill sweeping the yard.'

The miller's daughter was a good, devout girl, and she lived a God-fearing, virtuous life for those three years. When her time was up, and the day came for the Evil One to fetch her, she washed until she was clean and pure and drew a chalk circle around herself.

The Devil arrived early in the morning, but he couldn't get near her. He told the miller angrily, 'Take all the water away from her, so that she can't wash herself, for otherwise I have no power over her.'

The miller was frightened, and did as he was told. Next morning the Devil came back, but the girl had shed tears on her hands, and they were clean and pure. Yet again, the Devil couldn't get near her, and he angrily told the miller, 'Cut her hands off, for otherwise I can't touch her.'

The horrified miller replied, 'How can I cut off my own child's hands?'

Then the Evil One threatened him, saying, 'If you don't do it you're mine, and it will be you I take.'

The girl's father was afraid, and he promised to do as the Devil said. Then he went to the girl and said, 'My child, if I don't cut off both your hands the Devil will take me away with him, and in my fear I told him I'd do it. Help me in my hour of need, and forgive me for the terrible thing I must do.'

She said, 'Dear Father, do whatever you like to me. I am your child.' Then she held out both hands and let him chop them off. The Devil came for the third time, but she had wept so long and so hard over the stumps of her hands that they were pure and clean. So he had to own himself defeated, for he had lost all rights to her.

'Through you,' the miller told his daughter, 'I have won such riches that I will care for you and give you the best of everything all your life.'

But she said, 'I can't stay here, I want to go away. Kind people will give me all I need.' So she had her mutilated arms tied behind her back, and at sunrise she set out and walked all day until nightfall. Then she came to a royal garden, and in the moonlight she saw trees laden with beautiful fruit, but she couldn't get to them, because there was a moat full of water round the garden. She had been walking all day without a bite to eat, so now she was tormented by hunger, and she thought, oh, if only I were in the garden so that I could eat some of that fruit! I shall pine away and die without it! Then she knelt down, called on God's name and said her prayers. Suddenly an angel came down and closed a sluice in the water, so that the moat dried up and she could get across it. Now she entered the garden, and the angel went with her. She saw a tree covered with fruit – beautiful pears, but they had all been counted. She went over to them, tilted her mouth up to one and ate it from the tree to satisfy her hunger, but only one. The gardener saw her, but because the angel was standing beside her he was afraid and thought the girl was a ghost. He kept quiet and dared not call out or speak to her. When she had eaten the pear she felt better, and went to hide in the bushes.

The king who owned the garden came down to it next morning. He counted the fruits, saw that one pear was missing, and asked the gardener what had become of it; it wasn't lying under the tree, yet it was gone.

'Last night,' said the gardener, 'a ghost came into the garden. The ghost had no hands and ate the pear with only its mouth.'

'How did this ghost cross the water?' said the king. 'And where

did it go when it had eaten the pear?'

The gardener said, 'Someone came down from heaven in a snow-white robe, closed the sluice and kept the water back, so that the ghost could cross the moat. I was afraid, because it must have been an angel, so I asked no questions and didn't call out. When the ghost had eaten the pear it went away again.'

'If all you say is true,' replied the king, 'I will keep watch with you tonight myself.'

So when darkness fell the king came back to the garden, bringing a priest with him to speak to the ghost. All three of them sat down under the tree and kept watch. At midnight the girl came out of the bushes, went over to the tree and ate another pear with her mouth, while the white-robed angel stood beside her.

Then the priest went over to her and said, 'Do you come from God or are you of this world? Are you a ghost or a human being?'

She replied, 'I am not a ghost, only a poor girl abandoned by everyone but God.'

'You may be abandoned by all the world,' said the king, 'but I will not abandon you.' So he took her into his royal palace with him, and because she was so beautiful and good he fell deeply in love with her, had silver hands made for her, and took her as his wife.

After a year the king had to go away to war, and he gave the young queen into his mother's care, saying, 'When she has her baby, look after her well, and write me a letter at once to tell me.'

Well, the queen had a fine son, and the king's old mother was quick to write to her son and tell him the glad news. But the messenger carrying the letter stopped by a brook on his way to rest, and since he was tired after his long journey he fell asleep. Then the Devil came by, still trying to harm the good queen, so he exchanged the letter for another saying that she had brought a changeling into the world. When the king read that letter he was afraid, and very sad, but he wrote back to his mother telling her to look after the queen well and care for her until his return. The messenger took this letter back, stopped to rest at the same place, and fell asleep again. Then the Devil came by once more and put another letter in his bag, saying that the queen and her baby were to be killed. The king's old mother was horrified when she read those words. She couldn't believe what the letter said, and wrote back to the king again, but she received the same answer, because the Devil gave the messenger a false letter once more, and the last one said that the queen's tongue and eyes were to be kept as proof that she was dead.

But the king's old mother wept to think of shedding such innocent blood. She had a deer brought to the palace by night and slaughtered, cut out its eyes and tongue and kept them. Then she told the queen, 'I can't kill you as the king orders, but you cannot stay here any longer. You must go out into the world with your child and never come back.' She tied the baby on the queen's back, and the poor woman went away, weeping bitterly.

She came to a great, wild forest, where she knelt down and prayed to God, and the angel of the Lord appeared to her and led her to a little house with a sign on it saying, 'All may live here freely.' A maiden dressed in white came out of the little house, said, 'Welcome, my lady queen,' and took her in. The maiden untied the little boy from her back and held him to her breast, so that he could drink her milk, and then put him to sleep in a pretty little bed made up for him.

'How did you know I am a queen?' asked the poor woman.

The maiden in white replied, 'I am an angel sent by God to look after you and your baby.'

The queen spent seven years in that house, where she was well cared for, and she was so good that by the grace of God her hands grew again, even though they had been cut off.

At last the king came home from the wars, and his first thought was to see his wife and the child. Then his old mother began to shed tears. 'You wicked man!' she said. 'Why did you write telling me to take the lives of two innocent souls?' She showed him the two letters that the Evil One had forged, and went on, 'I did as you commanded,' and showed him the deer's eyes and tongue as proof.

The king himself began to weep even more bitterly for his poor wife and his little son, so that his old mother took pity on him and told him, 'Never fear, she is still alive. I had a deer slaughtered secretly and kept its eyes and tongue as a sign, but I tied the baby on your wife's back and told her to go out into the wide world. She had to promise never to come back again, because you were so angry with her.'

Then the king said, 'I will go to the ends of the earth, I will not eat or drink until I have found my dear wife and my child again, if they haven't died or perished of starvation by now.'

So saying, the king set off and went on his travels for seven long years, looking for his wife in every stony place and every cave in the rocks, but he didn't find her, and he thought she must have pined away and died. He didn't eat or drink in all this time, but God kept him alive. At last he came to a great forest and found the little house and the sign with the words saying, 'All may live here freely.' The maiden dressed in white came out, took him by the hand, led him into the house, said, 'Welcome, my lord king,' and asked where he came from.

'I have been on my travels for seven years,' he said, 'searching for my wife and child, but I cannot find them.'

The angel offered him food and drink, but he wouldn't take it, and asked only to rest a while. Then he lay down to sleep and covered his face with a cloth.

Next the angel went into the room where the queen was sitting with her son, whom she usually called Pain-Rich, and said to her, 'Come out and bring your child. Your husband is here.'

So the queen went over to him where he lay, and the cloth fell from his face. At that she said, 'Pain-Rich, pick up that cloth and cover your father's face again.'

The child picked it up, and covered the king's face. In his sleep the king heard it, and let the cloth fall again. At that the child became impatient, and said, 'Dear Mother, how can I cover my father's face? I have no father in this world. I have learnt to pray, "Our Father, that art in heaven", because you said the Lord God was our father, but how can I be expected to know a wild man like this? He's no father of mine.'

When the king heard that he sat up and asked who she was. She said, 'I am your wife, and this is your son Pain-Rich.'

But he saw her hands of flesh and blood, and said, 'My wife had silver hands.'

'By God's grace, my own hands have grown back again,' she replied, and the angel went into the other room, fetched the silver hands and showed them to him.

Then he knew for sure that this was his beloved wife, and the boy was his dear son, and he kissed them and was glad. 'Oh, what a weight has fallen from my heart!' he said.

The angel gave them food and drink, and afterwards they went home to the king's old mother. There was great rejoicing, the king and queen celebrated their wedding all over again, and they lived happily for the rest of their days.

Translator's note: This strange and eerie tale was probably first told to the Grimms by Marie Hassenpflug for the first edition of their collection, and Dorothea Viehmann added some details for the next edition. Folklore contains many superstitions about the Devil, and several feature here. The false message sent to the heroine's husband accusing her of killing her baby, or in this case of bringing a changeling into the world, is a widespread fairy-tale theme. It is often sent by a jealous mother-in-law, but here the old queen is a good character and saves the young woman and her baby. The Christian elements in the story are likely to be late additions.

The
Drummer

ne evening a young drummer was walking through the fields by himself, and when he came to a lake he saw three pieces of white linen lying on its banks. What fine linen, he said to himself, and he put one of the pieces in his pocket. He went home, thought no more of his find, and lay down in his bed.

But as he was about to fall asleep, it seemed to him that he heard someone calling his name. Listening, he caught the sound of a soft voice saying, 'Drummer, drummer, wake up.'

It was night, and pitch dark, so he couldn't see anyone, but he felt as if a figure were hovering up and down at his bedside.

'What do you want?' he asked.

'Give me my shift back again,' replied the voice, 'the shift you took from me yesterday evening by the lake.'

'You shall have it,' said the drummer, 'if you tell me who you are.'

'Oh,' replied the voice, 'I am the daughter of a mighty king, but I fell into the power of a witch, and now I'm banished to the glass mountain. I have to bathe in the lake with my two sisters every day, but without my shift I can't fly away again. My sisters have left, but I had to stay behind. Please give me my shift back.'

'Calm down, you poor child,' said the drummer. 'Of course I'll give it back.' And he brought it out of his pocket and handed it to her in the darkness. She quickly seized it and was about to go away.

'Wait a moment,' he said. 'Perhaps I can help you.'

'The only way to help me is to climb the glass mountain and free me from the witch's power. But you'll never find your way to

the glass mountain, and even if you were quite close to it you couldn't climb it.'

'When I want to do something, I can do it,' said the drummer. 'I'm sorry for you and I am not afraid of anything. But I don't know the way to the glass mountain.'

'It leads through the great forest where the man-eating ogres live. That's all I can tell you.' And then he heard her flying away.

At daybreak the drummer set off. He slung his drum around him and marched fearlessly into the forest. When he had been walking for some time, and hadn't seen any sign of a giant, he thought, these giants sleep late, I'd better wake them up. And he brought the drum round in front of him and played a drum-roll that made the birds fly out of the trees, screeching.

Before long a giant who had been lying asleep in the grass rose to his feet, and he was as tall as a spruce tree. 'You rascal,' shouted the giant, 'what are you doing here beating that drum and waking me from my beauty sleep?'

'I'm beating my drum,' he replied, 'because there are thousands of men coming along after me, and it's up to me to show them the way.'

'What are they doing here in my forest?' asked the giant.

'They're going to send you packing and rid the forest of such a monster.'

'Oh, are they indeed?' said the giant. 'I'll crush the whole lot of you underfoot like ants.'

'Do you think you can defeat them?' asked the drummer. 'If you bend down to seize one he'll run away and hide, but when you lie down to sleep they'll all come out of the bushes and climb up on you. Every man of them has a steel hammer at his belt, and they'll use those hammers to knock your skull in.'

The giant was downcast, and he thought, if I stop to deal with these cunning folk, I may get my skull knocked in. I can throttle wolves and bears, but I can't protect myself from earthworms like these.

'Listen, little fellow,' he told the drummer, 'go away again, will you? I promise to leave you and your friends alone in future, and if there's anything else you'd like, just tell me, and I'll be happy to do you a favour.'

'You have long legs,' said the drummer, 'you can walk faster than me, so if you carry me to the glass mountain I'll send my friends a signal telling them to retreat, and they'll leave you in peace this time.'

'Come here, little worm,' said the giant. 'Sit on my shoulder, and I'll carry you wherever you want.'

So the giant picked the drummer up, and once he was high up there he began beating his drum to his heart's content. That must be the signal for the rest of his men to retreat, thought the giant.

After a while they met a second giant along their way. He took the drummer from the first giant and put him in his buttonhole. The drummer took hold of the button, which was as big as a bowl, clung fast to it, and looked around him at his leisure. Then they came to a third giant, who took him from the second giant's buttonhole and put him on top of his hat. The drummer walked up and down there and looked across the treetops, and when he saw a mountain in the blue distance he thought, that must be the glass mountain. And so it was.

The giant took just a couple of steps more, and they had reached the foot of the mountain, where the giant put the drummer down. He asked to be carried to the top of the mountain too, but the giant shook his head, muttered something into his beard, and went back into the forest.

So there stood the poor drummer looking at the mountain, which was as high as three ordinary mountains one on top of the other and as smooth as a mirror, and he had no idea how to get up it. He began climbing, but that was no use; he kept sliding down again. If only I were a bird, he thought, but wishing did no good. He couldn't grow wings. As he stood there, at his wits' end, he saw two men not far away having a violent argument. He went towards them, and found that they were quarrelling about a saddle that lay on the ground in front of them. Each of them wanted to have it.

'What fools you are!' he said. 'Why quarrel over a saddle when you have no horse to put it on?'

'That saddle is well worth quarrelling for,' replied one of the men. 'Anyone who sits on it and wishes to be somewhere else, even at the other end of the world, will be there the moment he has uttered his wish. The saddle belongs to both of us, and it's my turn to ride on it, but that man there won't let me.'

'I can soon settle your argument,' said the drummer. He walked some way off and stuck a white staff into the ground. Then he came back and said, 'Now, both of you run to that mark, and whoever reaches it first gets the first ride.'

The two men set off to race each other, but they had hardly taken

a couple of steps before the drummer sat astride the saddle, wished himself on the glass mountain, and there he was in the twinkling of an eye.

There was a plain on top of the mountain, an old stone house stood on the plain, a large fish pond lay in front of the house and a dark forest grew behind it. The drummer saw neither man nor beast; all was still except for the wind rustling in the trees, and the drifting clouds not far above his head. He went up to the door and knocked. When he had knocked three times an old woman with a brown face and red eyes opened the door. She had a pair of glasses on the end of her long nose, and she looked keenly at him before asking what he wanted.

'Shelter, food, and a bed for the night,' replied the drummer.

'You shall have them,' said the old woman, 'if you will perform three tasks for me in return.'

'Why not?' he replied. 'I don't fear any tasks, however difficult.'

So the old woman let him in, gave him a meal and a good bed for the night. Next morning, when he had slept well, the old woman took a thimble off her thin finger, handed it to the drummer, and said, 'Now get to work scooping the water out of the fish pond with this thimble, but you must have it drained by nightfall, and all the fish in the water must be sorted into their species and size and laid side by side.'

'This is a strange task,' said the drummer, but he went out to the pond and began scooping out the water. He scooped all morning, but what use is a thimble for emptying a large stretch of water, even if you scooped for a thousand years?

At midday he thought, there's no point in this, and it's all the same whether I work or not. So he stopped and sat down. Then a girl came out of the house, brought him a little basket of food, and said, 'You look so sad sitting there. What's the matter?'

He looked at her, and saw that she was very beautiful. 'Oh,' he said, 'I can't finish the first task, so how can I ever perform the others? I set out to look for a princess who is said to live here, but I haven't found her, so I'll go on my way.'

'Stay here,' said the girl. 'I'll help you in your need. You are tired, so lay your head in my lap and sleep. When you wake up the task will be done.'

The drummer didn't have to be asked twice. As soon as his eyes were closed, the girl turned a wishing-ring on her finger and said, 'Water rise, fish come out.' The water immediately rose in the air like white mist and drifted away with the other clouds, and the fish, snapping for air, jumped up on the bank and lay down side by side in order of their size and species. When the drummer woke up, he was amazed to see that it had all been done.

The girl told him, 'One of those fish is not with its own kind, but all on its own. When the old woman comes this evening, and sees that

you've performed her task, she will say, "But what's that fish doing all alone?" Then you must throw the fish in her face and say, "That's for you, old witch."'

In the evening the old woman came, and when she had asked the question he threw the fish in her face. She acted as if she hadn't noticed, and said nothing, but she looked at him with an evil glint in her eyes.

Next morning she said, 'You had too easy a task yesterday. I must give you a harder one. You are to cut down all the trees in the forest, split the timber into logs, stack it up in woodpiles, and it must all be done by evening.' She gave him an axe, a hatchet and two wedges. But the axe was made of lead, and the hatchet and wedges were only tin. When he began chopping, the blade of the axe bent and the hatchet and wedges crumpled. He was at a loss, but at midday the girl came with food again and comforted him.

'Lay your head in my lap,' she said, 'go to sleep, and when you wake up the work will be done.'

She turned her wishing-ring, and as she did so the whole forest collapsed with a great crash, the timber split of its own accord, and it stacked itself up in woodpiles. It was as if invisible giants were doing the work. When the drummer woke up, the girl said, 'There, as you can see, the wood is split and stacked. There's just one

branch left over, and when the old woman comes this evening and asks what it's doing on its own, you must strike her with it and say, "That's for you, old witch."'

The old woman came in the evening. 'Well,' she said, 'you see how easy the task was, but why is that branch still lying alone there?'

'It's for you, old witch,' he replied, striking her with it. She acted as if she hadn't felt the blow, laughed scornfully and said, 'Tomorrow you are to gather all the wood into one big pile, set fire to it and burn it.'

He rose at daybreak, and began gathering the wood together, but how can one man carry the timber of all the trees in a forest? He was getting nowhere. But the girl didn't let him down: she brought him his meal at midday, and when he had eaten it he laid his head in her lap and went to sleep. When he woke up the whole great woodpile was burning fiercely, with tongues of flame licking up to the sky.

'Listen to me,' said the girl. 'When the witch comes she will ask you to do all kinds of things. Do whatever she says without fear and then she can't touch you. But if you are afraid, the flames will seize you and consume you. Finally, when you have done all she asks, seize her in both hands and throw her into the middle of the fire.'

The girl went away, and along came the old woman. 'Oh, how cold I am!' she said. 'But here's a fire burning to warm my old bones, and that will do me good. I see a log that won't burn there – just fetch it out for me. Once you've done that you are free to go where you like. In you jump!'

The drummer didn't stop to think twice, but jumped into the middle of the flames, and they didn't hurt him. They couldn't even singe his hair. He fetched the log out and put it down. But no sooner had the wood touched the ground than it changed shape, and there stood the beautiful girl who had helped him when he was in need. Her silken clothes, glittering with gold, showed him that she was the princess.

However, the old woman laughed nastily and said, 'You think you have her now, but oh no, not yet!' She was about to make for the girl and haul her away, but the drummer seized the old woman in both hands, raised her in the air and threw her into the jaws of the fire itself. They closed over her, as if they were glad to have a witch to eat.

Then the princess looked at the drummer, and when she saw that he was a handsome young man, and she remembered how he had risked his life to set her free, she gave him her hand and said, 'You have dared everything for me, and I'll do the same for you. Promise to be true to me, and you shall be my husband. We won't lack for wealth; what the witch has here will be plenty for us.'

She took him into the house, where the coffers were full of the witch's treasures. They left the gold and silver, and just took the jewels. The princess didn't want to stay on the glass mountain any longer, so the drummer told her, 'Sit on my saddle behind me and we'll fly down like birds.'

'I don't like that old saddle,' she said. 'I only have to turn the wishing-ring on my finger and it will take us home.'

'Very well,' replied the drummer. 'Take us to the city gates, then.'

They were there in the twinkling of an eye, and the drummer said, 'First of all I want to go and see my parents and give them our news. Wait for me here outside the town, and I'll soon be back.'

'Oh, please be careful,' said the princess. 'When you arrive, don't kiss your parents on the right cheek, or you will forget everything, and I'll be left alone and forlorn out here.'

'How could I forget you?' he said, and he promised her faithfully to be back very soon.

When he came to his parents' house, he had changed so much that no one recognised him, for the three days he had spent on the glass mountain had really been three long years. Then he told them who he was, and his mother and father embraced him with delight, and he was so moved that he didn't stop to think of what the girl had said, and he kissed them on both cheeks. But when he had kissed them on the right cheek he forgot all about the princess. He emptied his pockets and put handfuls of the biggest jewels ever seen on the table. His parents hardly knew what to do with all these riches, but his father built a magnificent castle surrounded by gardens, woods and meadows, a palace fit for a prince. And when it was finished, his mother said, 'I've chosen a girl for you to marry, and the wedding will be in three days' time.' The drummer agreed to everything his parents wanted.

The poor princess had stood outside the city

gates for a long time, waiting for the young man to return. When evening came, she said, 'I'm sure he has kissed his parents on the right cheek and forgotten me.' Her heart was so full of grief that she wished for a lonely little house in the woods to live in, and didn't want to go back to her father's court. Every evening she went into the town and walked past the drummer's house. Sometimes he saw her, but he didn't know who she was.

At last she heard people saying, 'His wedding festivities begin tomorrow.' Then she said to herself: I'll see if I can win his heart back.

When the first day of the festivities came, she turned her wishing-ring and said, 'I want a dress as bright as the sun.' Immediately the dress lay before her, as dazzling as if it had been woven of pure sunbeams. Once all the wedding guests had assembled, she stepped into the hall. They marvelled at the beautiful dress, and the drummer's bride marvelled most of all. Since she loved fine clothes more than anything else, she went up to the stranger and asked if she would sell the dress.

'Not for money,' replied the princess, 'but if I can spend the first night of the wedding outside the door of the room where the bridegroom sleeps, I'll let you have it.'

Well, the bride couldn't control her desire for the dress and agreed, but she mixed a sleeping draught in the wine that the bridegroom was to drink last thing at night, and he fell into a deep sleep. When all was quiet, the princess, crouching outside his bedroom door, opened it a little way and called:

'Drummer, drummer, hear me now.
Remember me, your promised wife.
From the witch I saved your life.
On the glassy hill sat we
When your faith you pledged to me.
Drummer, drummer, hear me now.'

But it was all in vain. The drummer didn't wake, and when morning came the princess had to go away without getting what she wanted.

On the second evening she turned her wishing-ring and said, 'I want a dress as silvery as the moon.' When she appeared at the wedding festivities in a dress as delicate as moonlight, the bride longed for this one too, and in return for it she allowed the princess to spend a second night outside the door of the bridegroom's room. In the silence of the night she called:
'Drummer, drummer, hear me now.
Remember me, your promised wife.
From the witch I saved your life.
On the glassy hill sat we
When your faith you pledged to me.
Drummer, drummer, hear me now.'

But the drummer's senses were dulled by the sleeping draught he had drunk, and the princess couldn't wake him. In the morning, she went sadly back to her little house in the woods.

However, the servants in the drummer's house had heard the stranger weeping and wailing, and they told the bridegroom about it, telling him that he couldn't have heard anything himself because they had been given instructions to put a sleeping draught in his wine.

On the third evening the princess turned the wishing-ring on her finger and said, 'I want a dress that sparkles like the stars.' When she came to the wedding festivities in it, the bride was amazed by the splendour of the dress, which far outshone the first two, and she said, 'I must and will have it.'

The girl said she would give it to her, like the other two, in return for permission to spend the night outside the bridegroom's door. But on this third night he didn't drink the wine he was given before going to sleep, and poured it out behind the bed instead. And when everything in the house had fallen still, he heard a soft voice calling to him:

'Drummer, drummer, hear me now.
Remember me, your promised wife.
From the witch I saved your life.
On the glassy hill sat we
When your faith you pledged to me.
Drummer, drummer, hear me now.'

Suddenly his memory came back to him. 'Oh,' he cried, 'how could I have been so faithless? It's all because of the kiss I gave my parents on the right cheek in the gladness of my heart – it took my memory away.' And he jumped up, took the princess by the hand and led her to his parents' bed.

'This is my true bride,' he said, 'and if I marry the other girl I shall be doing very wrong.'

When his parents heard how it had all happened they agreed. So the lights in the great hall were lit again, trumpets and drums were sent for, their friends and relations were invited to come back, and the real wedding was held with great rejoicing. As for the other bride, she was given the beautiful dresses as compensation, and she was happy with that.

Translator's note: *Here is another 'glass mountain' story, and you might like to compare it with 'The Iron Stove'. This time it is the hero of the story who uses magic to get to the top. But then, another frequent theme in fairy tales: he falls victim to a spell that makes him forget the resourceful girl who had helped them both to escape the witch. The three beautiful dresses worn by the heroine, and her bargain with the drummer's false bride to spend a night in his room trying to revive his memory, are themes that appear in many fairy tales.*

Mother Holle

There was once a widow who had two daughters, one of them beautiful and hard-working, the other ugly and lazy. But she loved the ugly, lazy girl much better than the good girl, because she was her own daughter, so her stepdaughter had to do all the work and was the household drudge. The poor girl was made to sit by a well at the roadside every day, spinning yarn until her fingers bled.

One day the bobbin of yarn was all bloodstained too, so the girl bent down to the well to wash it, but the bobbin fell out of her hands and into the water. Weeping, she ran to her stepmother and told her about the accident. The widow scolded her angrily, and said severely, 'Since you dropped the bobbin into the well you can fetch it out again yourself.'

So the girl went back to the well, at her wits' end, and in her terror she jumped right into it to fetch the bobbin out. She fainted away, and when she came back to her senses she was in a beautiful meadow where the sun shone and a thousand flowers grew. She walked on through this meadow and came to an oven full of bread. The bread called, 'Oh, take me out, take me out or I'll burn; I was baked long ago.' So she went up to the oven and took all the loaves out with the bread shovel.

After that she went on and came to a tree covered with apples, and the tree called, 'Oh, shake me, shake me, we apples are all ripe.' So she shook the tree and made the apples fall like rain. She went on shaking until there wasn't an apple left on the branches, and when she had gathered the apples all together in a heap she walked on again.

At last she came to a little house. An old woman was looking out of the window, but because she had such big teeth the girl was frightened, and was going to hurry on. However, the old woman called after her, 'What are you afraid of, dear child? Stay with me, and if you'll keep house for me nicely you'll be well off. You must just take care to make my bed properly and shake it thoroughly to make the feathers fly, because I'm Mother Holle and that's when snow falls in the world.'

Hearing the old woman speak to her so kindly, the girl plucked up her courage, agreed, and entered Mother Holle's service. She did everything to her mistress's satisfaction, and always shook her bed properly, making the feathers fly around like snowflakes. In return she lived very well with the old lady, who never said a cross word to her, and she had stewed and roast meat to eat every day. Well, after she had spent some time with Mother Holle she began to feel sad, she herself wasn't sure why at first, but in the end she realised that she was homesick. Although she was a thousand times better off here than at home, she still longed to go back. At last she told the old woman, 'I'm grieving for my home, and though you treat me so well down here, I can't stay any longer. I must go back up to my own people.'

Mother Holle said, 'I'm glad to hear that you want to go home, and since you have served me so faithfully I'll take you back to the world above myself.' So saying, she took her by the hand and led her to a great gateway. The gate was opened, and as the girl stood in the gateway a great shower of gold rained down on her, and all the gold clung to her and covered her all over. 'That's for you, because you have worked so hard,' said Mother Holle, and she also gave the girl back the bobbin that had fallen down the well. Then the gate was closed, and the girl found herself back in the world above, not far from her mother's house. When she came into the yard, the rooster sitting on the well crowed:

'Cock-a-doodle-do, cock-a-doodle-do,
Our golden girl's come home again, cock-a-doodle-do.'

Then she went indoors, and since she had come home covered with gold her stepmother and stepsister welcomed her kindly.

The girl told them everything that had happened to her, and when the mother heard how she had come by all those riches, she wanted her other daughter, the ugly, lazy girl, to get the same good fortune. She had to sit by the well and spin, and to make her bobbin bloody she pricked her finger and thrust her hand into a thorny hedge. Then she threw the bobbin into the well and jumped in after it herself.

Like her sister, she came to the beautiful meadow and walked along the same path. When she reached the oven the bread called: 'Oh, take me out, take me out or I'll burn; I was baked long ago.'

But she replied, 'Do you think I want to make myself all dirty?' And she walked on.

Soon she reached the apple tree, and the tree called, 'Oh, shake me, shake me, we apples are all ripe.'

But she replied, 'What an idea! One of the apples might fall on my head.' And she walked on.

When she came to Mother Holle's house she wasn't afraid, because she had already heard about her big teeth, and she immediately agreed to serve the old woman. On the first day she made herself work hard, and obeyed Mother Holle when she asked her to do something, because she kept thinking of all the gold she would be given. On the second day, however, she began to be idle, and the third day was even worse, for she wouldn't get up in the morning. She didn't make Mother Holle's bed properly either, and wouldn't shake it until the feathers flew. So Mother Holle soon grew tired of her, and told her to leave her service.

The lazy girl was glad of that, thinking that now the time for the shower of gold had come. Mother Holle led her to the gate, but when she was standing in the gateway a large cauldron full of pitch was tipped over her instead of the gold. 'That's the reward for your services,' said Mother Holle, and she closed the gate.

So the lazy girl went home, covered with pitch, and when the rooster on the well saw her he crowed:
'Cock-a-doodle-do, cock-a-doodle-do
Our dirty girl's come home again, cock-a-doodle do.'

As for the pitch, it stuck to her and wouldn't come off as long as she lived.

__Translator's note:__ Dorothea Wild, then aged eighteen, told the Grimms this story in which kindness is rewarded, while the lazy sister who tries taking a short cut to good fortune suffers for it. Jacob Grimm thought that 'Mother Holle' herself was originally a pre-Christian Germanic goddess.

The Wishing-Table, the Gold-Donkey and the Cudgel in the Sack

Once upon a time there was a tailor who had three sons, and they owned a single goat whose milk had to feed them all. So the goat needed good fodder, and she was taken out to pasture every day. The sons took turns looking after her. One day the eldest son took her out to the churchyard where the best grass grew, and let her graze and run about there. In the evening, when it was time to go home, he asked, 'Goat, have you had enough to eat?'

And the goat replied:

'That grass was a delicious treat.
Another blade I couldn't eat.
Bleat, bleat, bleat!'

'Come along home, then,' said the boy, and he took her halter, led her home and tied her up in the shed.

'Well,' said the old tailor, 'did the goat have good grazing?'

'Oh yes,' said his son, 'she said it was such a treat she couldn't eat another blade of grass.'

But the boy's father wanted to make sure, so he went down to the shed, patted the animal and asked, 'Goat, have you really had enough to eat?'

And the goat replied:

'All I could do in the churchyard was play.
I saw not a blade of grass all day.
So how would I get enough to eat?
Bleat, bleat, bleat!'

'What's all this?' cried the tailor, and he ran into the house and said to his son, 'Oh, you liar! You said the goat had good grazing, but you let her go hungry all day!' He was so angry that he took his yardstick off the wall where it was hanging and drove the boy out of the house with it.

Next day it was the second son's turn. He found a good place by the garden hedge where grass and herbs grew, and the goat ate them all.

In the evening, when it was time to go home, he asked, 'Goat, have you had enough to eat?'

And the goat replied:

'Those herbs were a delicious treat.
Another sprig I couldn't eat.
Bleat, bleat, bleat!'

'Come along home, then,' said the boy, and he took her back and tied her up in the shed.

'Well,' said the old tailor, 'did the goat have good grazing?'

'Oh yes,' said his son, 'she said it was such a treat that she couldn't eat another sprig of the herbs.'

But the tailor didn't trust his son, so he went down to the shed and asked, 'Goat, have you really had enough to eat?'

And the goat replied:

'All I could do by the bushes was play.
I found no grass or herbs all day.
So how would I get enough to eat?
Bleat, bleat, bleat!'

'Oh, the wicked boy!' cried the tailor. 'Letting such a good goat go hungry!' And he ran upstairs and drove the second son out of the house with his yardstick.

Now it was the third son's turn. He wanted to be sure the goat was well fed, so he looked for the bushes with the juiciest leaves and let the goat graze on them.

In the evening, when it was time to go home, he asked, 'Goat, have you had enough to eat?'

And the goat replied:

'Those leaves were a delicious treat.

Another leaf I couldn't eat.

Bleat, bleat, bleat!'

'Come along home, then,' said the boy, and he took her home and tied her up in the shed.

'Well,' said the old tailor, 'did the goat have good grazing?'

'Oh yes,' said his son, 'she said it was such a treat she couldn't eat another leaf.'

But the boy's father wanted to make sure, so he went down to the shed, patted the animal and asked, 'Goat, have you really had enough to eat?'

And the goat replied:

'All I could do in the bushes was play.
I had not a single leaf all day.
So how would I get enough to eat?
Bleat, bleat, bleat!'

'Oh, what liars they are!' cried the tailor. 'Each of you boys is as wicked and undutiful as the next! Well, you don't fool me any longer!' And beside himself with rage, he jumped up and beat the poor boy with his yardstick so hard that the lad ran out of the house and away.

So now the old tailor was alone with his goat. Next day he went down to the shed, patted the animal, and said, 'Come along, good little goat, I'm going to take you out to pasture myself.'

Leading her by the halter, he took her out to pasture where green hedges and yarrow grew, along with other plants that goats like to eat. 'There, you can eat your fill for once,' he told her, and he let her graze until evening. Then he asked: 'Goat, have you had enough to eat?'

And the goat replied:

'All that was a delicious treat.
Another plant I couldn't eat.
Bleat, bleat, bleat!'

'Come along home, then,' said the tailor, and he took her home and tied her up in the shed. As he was leaving, he turned and said, 'Well, at least you've had enough to eat this time!'

But the goat wasn't letting him off any more lightly than his sons, and she replied:

'All I could do out at pasture was play.
I saw no grass or leaves all day.
So how would I get enough to eat?
Bleat, bleat, bleat!'

When the tailor heard that, he was taken aback, and he saw that he had driven his three sons away for no reason at all. 'Just you wait, you ungrateful creature!' he cried. 'Chasing you away isn't punishment enough. I'll teach you not to show your face among honest tailors again!' And he ran upstairs, fetched his razor, soaped the goat's head and shaved it as smooth as the flat of his hand. Then, thinking his yardstick too good for her, he picked up a whip and lashed her until she ran away.

Now that the tailor was left all alone in his house he felt very sad, and he wished his sons were home again, but no one knew where they had gone. As it happened, the eldest son had apprenticed himself to a joiner. He soon learned the trade and worked hard, and when it was time for him to go on his travels as a journeyman his master gave him a little table. It didn't look anything special, and it was made of ordinary wood – but it had one remarkable quality. If you put it down on the ground and said, 'Little table, lay yourself!' the good little table was suddenly covered with a clean tablecloth, and on the cloth stood a plate with a knife and fork beside it, and as many dishes as there was room for. They were full of braised and roast meat, and there was a big glass of bright red wine to drink with your dinner and cheer your heart.

Well, thought the young journeyman, this table will provide for me all my life! So he travelled merrily around, and he never had to wonder whether an inn was good or bad, or whether he could even get a meal there at all. If he didn't feel like it he needn't go indoors, since he could just take his little table off his back out in the fields or the woods or in a meadow, anywhere he liked, put it down on the ground and say, 'Little table, lay yourself!' And next moment it was laden with everything his heart could desire.

After a while he decided to go back to his father, whose anger must have died down by now, and who would surely be glad to see him and his wonderful table. It so happened that one evening, on his way home, he went into an inn full of other guests. They welcomed him and invited him to share their meal, saying he'd have difficulty in getting anything to eat otherwise.

'No, no,' replied the joiner, 'I won't deprive you of any of your supper. Indeed, you must all be my guests instead!'

They laughed, thinking he was joking. But he put his little wooden table down in the middle of the room and said, 'Little table, lay yourself!' At once it was covered with food much better than anything the landlord of the inn could serve, and a most delicious smell rose to the guests' nostrils.

'Help yourselves, good friends,' said the joiner, and when the guests saw that he meant it they didn't wait to be asked twice but pulled up their chairs, took out their knives and ate a hearty meal. What surprised them most of all was to see that as soon as a dish was empty a full one appeared in its place, entirely of its own accord.

Now the landlord of the inn was standing in a corner, watching all this; he hardly knew what to say, but he thought to himself, I could do with a cook like that here!

The joiner and the rest of the company made merry until late into the night, when at last they lay down to sleep. The young journeyman put his little wishing-table beside the wall when he went to bed. But the landlord's thoughts wouldn't let him rest, and he remembered that he had an old table which looked just like the joiner's in his lumber room – so very quietly he carried it in, and exchanged it for the wishing-table.

Next morning the joiner paid for his night's rest, picked up his table, never dreaming that he might have the wrong one, and went on his way. At midday he came to his father's house, and the tailor was delighted to see him.

'Well, my dear son, what have you learned?' his father asked.

'I'm a joiner now, dear Father.'

'That's a good trade,' replied the old man. 'And what have you brought home from your travels?'

'The best thing I've brought home, dear Father, is this little table.'

The tailor looked at it from all sides and said, 'Well, that's no masterpiece! It's just an old table, and badly made at that.'

'Ah, but it's a wishing-table,' replied his son. 'If I put it down and tell it to lay itself, it's immediately covered with the most wonderful food, and wine to cheer your heart. So invite our friends and relations to come and eat and drink their fill, because this table will provide for them all.'

When the company arrived, he put his little table down in the middle of the room and said, 'Little table, lay yourself!' But the table didn't do anything at all, and stayed as empty as any other table that doesn't understand human language. At that the poor journeyman realised that his own table had been stolen, and he felt ashamed because now he looked like a liar. As for his relations, they laughed heartily, but they had to go home again without any food or drink. His father picked up his needle and his cloth and went on with his tailoring, and the son went to work for a master joiner living nearby.

The second son had apprenticed himself to a miller, and when his apprenticeship was over his master said, 'You've done well, so I'm giving you a very special donkey. But mind, he doesn't pull a cart, and he doesn't carry sacks.'

'Then what use is he?' asked the young journeyman miller.

'He spits gold, that's what,' replied the miller. 'If you stand him on a cloth and say, "Bricklebrit", then this good little donkey will shed gold pieces at both ends, from his mouth and his behind.'

'Well, what a fine donkey he is!' said the journeyman, and he thanked his master and went out into the world. When he needed gold, he had only to say 'Bricklebrit' to his donkey, and there was a shower of gold pieces. All he had to do was bend down and pick them up. Wherever he went on his travels nothing but the best was good enough for him, and the more expensive the better, because his purse was always full.

When he had been around the world for a while, he thought, it's time to go home and see my father – and if I bring the donkey who spits gold with me, he'll forget his anger and welcome me kindly.

Now it so happened that he stopped at the very same inn where the landlord had cheated his brother out of the little wishing-table. He was leading his donkey, and the landlord was going to take the animal from him and tie it up, but the young journeyman miller said, 'Don't trouble yourself. I'll take my grey friend here to the stable and tie him up myself. I have to know just where he is.'

Well, this seemed strange to the landlord, and he thought that a man who had to look after his own donkey wouldn't have much money to spend. But when, to his amazement, the stranger put his hand in his pocket, brought out two gold pieces and told him to get something good for his supper, the landlord hurried off to find the very best that money could buy.

After supper his guest asked what he owed, and the landlord decided to charge double the proper price and demanded two more gold pieces. The journeyman put his hand in his pocket, but he had run out of gold.

'Wait a minute, landlord,' said he. 'I'll just go and get some more money.' And he took the tablecloth with him. The landlord had no idea what that might be for, but he felt curious, so he followed in secret, and when his guest bolted the stable door he peered through a knothole in the wood. The stranger spread out the cloth under the donkey's hooves, said, 'Bricklebrit', and at once a shower of gold came out of the animal at both ends. Gold pieces fairly rained down on the ground.

'My word!' said the landlord. 'That's a good way of coining money! I wouldn't mind a purse of gold like this donkey for myself!'

The guest paid what he owed and lay down to sleep, but during the night the landlord went down to the stable, led away the donkey that could spit gold pieces, and tied up another donkey in its place.

Early next morning the journeyman miller set off with the donkey, thinking it was still his own donkey, the one that could spit gold. At midday he reached his father's house. The tailor was delighted to see him again, and welcomed him in.

'So what's become of you, my son?' asked the old tailor.

'I'm a miller now, dear Father,' said the young man.

'And what have you brought back from your travels?'

'Only a donkey.'

There are more than enough donkeys around here,' said his father. 'I'd rather have had a good goat.'

'Ah,' said the son, 'but this is no ordinary donkey. He's a gold-donkey – when I say "Bricklebrit", that good little animal will shed enough gold pieces to cover a whole cloth. Just ask our relations to come and visit us, and I'll make them all rich.'

'I like the sound of that,' said the tailor. 'Then I can put my needle and thread away and stop work!' And he himself hurried around inviting their relations to visit. As soon as they had all assembled, the miller told them to stand back, and then he spread out his cloth and led the donkey into the room.

'Now, watch this!' said the young miller, and he called, 'Bricklebrit!' But what came out of the donkey wasn't gold, and showed that the animal didn't know the trick of it, as indeed not every donkey does. Well, the poor miller looked very downcast, seeing that he'd been cheated, and he apologised to the family, who went home as poor as they had come. There was nothing for it, the old man had to go back to his needle and thread, and his son found work with a local miller.

The third brother had apprenticed himself to a turner, and because that's a highly skilled trade his apprenticeship was the longest. But his brothers sent him a letter, telling him about their bad luck and how the landlord of the inn had cheated them of their wonderful gifts the evening before they came home. When the turner had learned his trade and was about to set out on his travels, his master gave him a sack as a present for doing so well, and said, 'There's a cudgel in that sack.'

'I can sling the sack around me,' said the young man, 'and I'm sure it will be very useful, but what good is the cudgel? It will only weigh the sack down.'

'I'll tell you what use it is,' said the master turner. 'If anyone harms you, then you have only to say, "Out of the sack, cudgel", and that cudgel will fly around beating the man who means you ill, leading him such a merry dance that he won't be able to move for a week, and it won't stop until you say, "Back in the sack, cudgel!"'

The journeyman turner thanked him, slung the sack around him, and when anyone came too close and looked like attacking him he said, 'Out of the sack, cudgel!' The cudgel would jump out at once and thump away on the attacker's coat or jacket, not even waiting for him to take it off first. It all happened so quickly that it was the next villain's turn before he knew it.

At evening the young turner came to the inn where his brothers had been tricked. He put his sack down on the table in front of him and began telling the company about all the wonderful things he had seen in the world. 'Oh yes,' said he, 'you may find a wishing-table that lays itself, a donkey that spits gold and suchlike, all very good things in their way and indeed I don't despise them, but they can't hold a candle to the treasure I've gained. I have it here with me in this sack.'

The landlord pricked up his ears. Aha, he thought, what in the world can the treasure be? I dare say that sack is full of jewels, and it's only right they should be mine, because all good things come in threes.

When it was time to go to sleep, the guest stretched out on a bench and put his sack under his head for a pillow. As soon as the landlord thought the young man was fast asleep, he went over and very gently and cautiously pulled and tugged at the sack, to see if he could get it out and leave another one there instead. This was just what the turner had been waiting for. When the landlord was about to give a final good tug, he cried, 'Out of the sack, cudgel!' And immediately the cudgel jumped out and began beating the landlord black and blue. The man yelled for mercy, but the louder he shouted the harder the cudgel kept time with his yells, thudding down on his back, until at last he fell to the floor exhausted.

'Now then,' said the turner, 'give me back the wishing-table and the donkey that spits gold, or we'll dance that dance all over again.'

'No, no!' cried the landlord, in a faint voice. 'I'll happily give it all back, only make that terrible demon go back inside the sack again!'

So the journeyman turner said, 'I'll show mercy as well as justice, but be careful what you do in future!' Then he said, 'Back in the sack, cudgel!' and let the cudgel rest.

Next morning the turner went home to his father with the wishing-table and the donkey that could shed gold. The tailor was very glad to see him, and asked him in his own turn what he had learned while he was away.

'Dear Father,' said the young man, 'I've become a turner.'

'That's a skilled trade,' said his father. 'And what have you brought back from your travels?'

'Something very valuable, dear Father,' replied his son. 'A cudgel in this sack.'

'What!' cried his father. 'A cudgel! That was hardly worth your while. You can cut a cudgel from any tree.'

'Not a cudgel like this one, dear Father. If I say, "Out of the sack, cudgel!" then the cudgel will jump out and lead anyone who means me harm a merry dance, and it won't stop beating him until he's lying on the ground begging for mercy. Look, this cudgel helped me to get back the wishing-table and the gold-donkey stolen from my brothers by that thieving landlord. So send for both my brothers and invite all our relations too. I want to give them a feast of good food and drink, and fill their pockets with gold.'

The old tailor could hardly believe his son's story, but he sent for his other two sons and all their relations. Then the turner spread a cloth on the floor of the room, led the donkey in, and told his brother the miller, 'Go on, dear brother, speak to him.'

'Bricklebrit,' said the miller, and at once a shower of gold pieces fell on the cloth. They might have been raining down from a cloudburst, and the donkey didn't stop until all the tailor's guests had so much gold in their pockets that they couldn't carry any more. (And I'm sure you'd have liked to be there yourself.)

Then the turner brought in the little table and told his brother the joiner, 'Dear brother, speak to it.' As soon as the joiner had said, 'Little table, lay yourself!' the table was covered with a cloth and richly laid with the finest of dishes. Then there was such a banquet as the good tailor had never seen in his house before, and all the family stayed until night, very merry and content. The tailor put his needle and thread, his yardstick and his smoothing iron away in a cupboard, and lived in joy and prosperity with his three sons.

But where did the goat go – the goat whose fault it was that the tailor turned his three sons out of doors? I'll tell you. She was ashamed of her shaven head, so she found a fox's earth and crawled into it. When the fox came home he saw a pair of large eyes glowing in the dark, and he was so frightened that he ran away again. Then the bear met him, and seeing how scared the fox looked he said, 'What's the matter, brother Reynard, why do you look like that?'

'Oh,' said Reynard the fox, 'there's a terrible creature in my earth, staring at me with its fiery eyes.'

'We'll soon drive it away,' said the bear, and he went to the earth and looked in, but when he saw the fiery eyes himself he was frightened too. He wanted nothing to do with the fierce creature, and took to his heels.

The bee met the bear, and when she saw how upset he was she said, 'Bear, you look terrible, and you're usually so cheerful. What's happened?'

'It's all very well for you to talk,' said the bear, 'but there's a dreadful creature with great goggling eyes in brother Reynard's earth, and we can't drive it out.'

'I feel sorry for you, Bear. I'm only a poor, weak little insect, and you and the fox wouldn't usually spare me a glance, but I believe I can help you.'

Then she flew into the fox's earth, settled on the goat's smooth, shaven head, and stung the goat so badly that the animal jumped up, bleating and bleating, ran out into the wide world like a creature run mad, and to this day nobody knows where she went.

Translator's note: Like 'The Bremen Town Band', this longer story is humorous, but there is plenty of magic in the shape of the wonderful powers of the objects in the title. Stories of this kind, in which three sons try to gain their father's favour, are widespread throughout the world, appearing, for instance, in the 'Thousand and One Nights'. Sometimes the brothers are competing to find a wonderful item, but in this case they all help each other, and the reader has the satisfaction of seeing honesty winning out over deception.

The Frog King

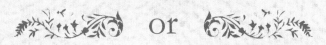

or

Iron Henry

In the old days, when wishes still came true, there was a king whose daughters were all beautiful, but the youngest princess was so lovely that the sun itself, although it had seen so much, was astonished when it shone on her face. There was a great dark forest near the king's castle, and a well stood there under an old linden tree. On very hot days the princess went into the forest and sat on the rim of the cool well, and when she was bored she would take out her golden ball, throw it up in the air and catch it again. That was her favourite game.

Well, one day it happened that when the princess held up her hands for the golden ball it didn't drop back into them, but fell on the ground beside her and rolled straight into the water. The princess followed the ball with her eyes, but it disappeared, and the well was deep, so deep that you couldn't see the bottom of it. Then she began to weep, and she wept louder and louder and could not console herself.

As she was weeping and wailing like this, someone called out to her and asked, 'What's the matter, princess? You're crying fit to melt a heart of stone.'

She looked round to see where the voice came from, and saw a frog putting its ugly great head out of the water. 'Oh, it's you, is it, old water-splasher?' she said. 'I'm sad because my golden ball has fallen into the well.'

'Hush, don't cry,' said the frog. 'I can help you, but what will you give me in return if I bring you back your toy?'

'Whatever you like, dear frog,' she said. 'My clothes, my pearls and precious stones, even the golden crown I wear.'

'I don't want your clothes, your pearls and precious stones or your golden crown,' replied the frog. 'But if you will love me, if you'll take me for your companion and playmate, let me sit beside you at your little table, eat from your little golden plate and drink from your little goblet, if you will let me sleep in your little bed – if you'll promise me all that, then I'll go down into the well and bring you up your golden ball again.'

'Oh yes,' she said, 'I'll promise anything you like if only you'll bring me back my ball.' But she thought to herself, what nonsense that silly frog talks! He lives in the water with other frogs, croaking. He can't be a human being's companion.

When she had given the frog her promise, he put his head under the water, dived right down, and after a little while he came paddling up again with the ball in his mouth and dropped it on the grass. The princess was overjoyed to see her beautiful toy again, and she picked it up and ran away with it.

'Wait, wait,' called the frog. 'Take me with you! I can't run as fast as you.' Loud as he croaked after her, however, it did him no good. She wasn't listening, but hurried home and soon forgot the poor frog, who had to climb down into his well again.

Next day, when she was sitting at table with the king and all his courtiers, eating from her little golden plate, something came hopping up the marble stairs, splish splosh, splish splosh, and when it had reached the top of the stairs it knocked on the door and cried, 'King's daughter, youngest king's daughter, open the door and let me in.' She went to see who was outside, and when she opened the door there sat the frog. Quickly, she slammed the door again and sat down at the table, feeling very frightened.

The king could see that her heart was thudding hard, and he said, 'What are you afraid of, my child? Is there a giant outside the door who wants to take you away?'

'Oh no,' she said, 'it's not a giant, only a nasty frog.'

'What does the frog want?'

'Oh, dear father, when I was sitting by the well in the forest yesterday, playing, my golden ball fell into the water. And I cried so

hard that the frog fetched it out again, and I promised that he could
be my companion, because that was what he said he wanted, but I
never thought he'd be able to leave the water in his well. Now he's
outside, asking to come in and join me.'

Then the frog knocked for the second time, calling:

'Youngest daughter of the king
Open the door and let me in.
Don't you remember the ball that fell
Into the water of the well?
Youngest princess, fair to see
Don't you remember your promise to me?
Youngest daughter of the king
Open the door and let me in.'

Then the king said, 'If you made a promise you must keep it, so go and let him in.'

She went to open the door, and the frog hopped in and followed her over to her chair. Then he sat on the floor, saying, 'Pick me up so that I can sit beside you.' She hesitated, but at last the king told her to pick the frog up. Once on her chair he wanted to be on the table, and when he was sitting on the table he said, 'Now push your little golden plate closer to me so that we can eat together.'

She did as he asked, but anyone could see she didn't like it. The frog ate a hearty meal, but she could hardly swallow a morsel. At last the frog said, 'I've eaten well and I'm tired, so carry me to your little bedroom, make your little bed up with silken sheets, and we'll lie down and go to sleep.'

The king's daughter began weeping, for she was afraid of the clammy frog. She didn't like to touch him, and now he was to sleep in her pretty little bed. But the king was angry, and he said, 'When someone has helped you in your time of need, you mustn't despise him afterwards.'

So she picked the frog up in her fingertips, carried him to her room and put him down in a corner. But when she was in bed he came hopping along and said, 'I'm tired, I want to sleep comfortably like you, so lift me up or I'll tell your father.'

Then she lost her temper, picked him up and threw him against the wall with all her might, saying, 'That'll keep you quiet, you nasty frog!'

However, when he fell to the floor he wasn't a frog any more, but a prince with kind and beautiful eyes. With her father's consent, he married her to be her dear husband and companion. The prince told her how a spell had been cast on him by a wicked witch, and she was the only one in the world who could release him from the well. Tomorrow, he said, they would go to his own kingdom. So they went to sleep, and when the sun woke them next morning a carriage came driving up, drawn by eight white horses, with plumes of white ostrich feathers on their heads, and golden harness, and the prince's servant Faithful Henry was standing up behind the carriage. Faithful Henry had been so sad when his master was turned into a frog that he had three iron bands forged round his heart, to keep it from breaking with sorrow and grief. Now the prince was going home to his kingdom, and Faithful Henry helped him and his wife into the carriage and got up behind it again, full of joy to see his master released from the spell.

When they had driven a little way the prince heard a crack behind him, like the sound of something breaking. So he turned round and called:

'Henry, the carriage is breaking.'
'No, sir, but my heart was aching,
When you were a frog and sat in the well
Under the wicked witch's spell.
Now one of the bands has broken again
From round my heart to ease the pain.'

There were two more cracks as they drove along, and both times the prince thought that the carriage was breaking, but the sound was only the bands round Faithful Henry's heart bursting because his master was happy and released from the spell.

Translator's note: *This is the very first story in the great collection of the Brothers Grimm, and it was probably given to them by Dorothea Wild, the family friend who married Wilhelm Grimm in 1825. In many other versions of this tale, the princess who learns that she must keep her promises has to kiss the frog before the spell on him is broken. Here she just throws him against the wall. There are versions of this story from all over the world, and it belongs to a large group known as 'animal bridegroom' stories, in which a girl must overcome her distaste and learn to be generous and unselfish before the enchanted animal turns into the man of her dreams. The extra little story of 'Iron Henry' is added at the end.*

The Goose-Girl

Once upon a time there was an old queen whose husband had died many years before, and she had a beautiful daughter. When the princess grew up, she was promised in marriage to a king's son who lived far away. So when the time came for her to be married, and she was to travel to the prince's distant kingdom, the old queen packed up many precious things for her to take: gold and silver-work; goblets and jewels; in short, all that should be part of a royal dowry, for she loved her daughter dearly. She sent a chambermaid to go with the bride too and deliver her safely to her bridegroom, and each of them had a horse to ride. The princess's horse was called Falada, and he could speak.

When the time came for mother and daughter to part, the old queen went to her bedroom, took a little knife and cut her finger until it bled. Then she held a white cloth under her hand and let three drops of blood fall on it, gave the cloth to her daughter and said, 'Dear child, keep this carefully. You will need it on your journey.'

So they sadly said goodbye to each other. The princess tucked the white cloth inside the breast of her dress, mounted her horse, and rode away to meet her bridegroom. When they had been riding for an hour she felt thirsty, and said to her chambermaid, 'Get off your horse, take the goblet you have brought for me, and bring me some water from the brook. I'd like a drink.'

'If you are thirsty,' said the chambermaid, 'get off your own horse, lie down by the water and drink. I'm not going to be your servant any more.'

So the princess, who was very thirsty indeed, dismounted, leaned over the water in the brook and drank, although she couldn't drink from her golden goblet. 'Oh, dear God!' she said. Then the three drops of blood answered her, saying, 'If your mother only knew, her heart would surely break in two.'

However, the princess was not a proud girl, and she said nothing, but mounted her horse again. So they rode on for several miles, but the day was hot, the sun burned down, and soon she was thirsty once more. As they were coming to a river, she asked her chambermaid again, 'Get down and give me water to drink in my golden goblet.' For she had long ago forgotten the girl's unkind words.

However, the chambermaid said even more haughtily, 'If you want to drink, drink by yourself. I'm not going to serve you any more.'

So the princess got down, being very thirsty, leaned over the flowing water, wept and said, 'Oh, dear God!' And the drops of blood answered her again, saying, 'If your mother only knew, her heart would surely break in two.' As she drank, bending far over the water, the little cloth with the three drops of blood fell out of her dress and floated away, and in her fear she never noticed. But the chambermaid had seen it fall, and was glad that she now had power over the young bride, because the loss of the three drops of blood had made her weak and drained all her strength away.

As the princess was about to remount the horse Falada, the chambermaid said, 'I'm the one who should ride Falada, and you must ride this old nag of mine.' The girl had to put up with that.

Then the chambermaid ordered her harshly to take off her royal clothes and put on her own shabby dress. Last of all she had to swear under the open sky that when they reached the prince's court she wouldn't tell a living soul what had happened, and if she hadn't sworn that oath she would have been killed on the spot. But the horse Falada saw and remembered everything.

Now the chambermaid mounted Falada, and the real bride got on the poorer horse, and so they rode on until at last they reached the royal castle. There were great rejoicings at their arrival, and the king's son ran to meet them and lifted the chambermaid down from her horse, thinking she was his promised wife. She was led up the stairs, while the real princess had to stand at the bottom of them.

Looking out of the window, the old king saw her standing in the yard, and noticing how fine, delicate and beautiful she was, he went straight to the royal apartments and asked the bride about the girl who had come with her and was now standing down in the yard.

'Oh, she's a maid I brought to keep me company on the way,' said the bride. 'Give the girl something to do, so that she doesn't stand about idle.'

But the old king had no work for her, and could think of nothing except to say, 'Well, I have a little lad who looks after the geese, she can help him.' The gooseherd's name was Curdie, and the real bride had to help him tend the geese.

Soon, however, the false bride told the prince, 'Dear husband, will you do me a favour?'

'With all my heart,' he said.

'Then send for the knacker to cut off the head of the horse I rode coming here, because he made me angry on the way.' But really she was afraid the horse might speak and say how she had treated the princess.

Now when the day came for the faithful Falada to die, the real princess heard about it, and she secretly promised the knacker money if he would do her a small service. There was a great dark gateway in the city, and she had to pass through it with the geese every morning and evening. She asked him to nail up Falada's head under the dark gateway, so that she could see him again, and more than once. The knacker promised to do as she asked, cut off the horse's head and nailed it under the dark gateway.

Early in the morning, when she and Curdie went out through the gate, she said as she passed:
'Alas, Falada, you hang there!'

And the head replied:
'Alas, you suffer grief and care.
If your mother only knew
Her heart would surely break in two.'

Then she walked quietly on out of the city, driving the geese to their pasture. And when she had reached the meadow she sat down and unbraided her hair, which was like pure gold. Curdie saw it, and liked the way it gleamed. He wanted to pull out a couple of her hairs, but she said:

> *'Wind, wind, blow today,*
> *Blow Curdie's hat away!*
> *Make the boy run after it.*
> *In the meantime here I'll sit*
> *Combing out my hair and then*
> *Braiding it all up again.'*

And such a strong wind rose that it swept Curdie's hat far away, and he had to run after it. By the time he came back she had finished

combing her hair and pinning up her braids, and he couldn't catch hold of a single hair. Curdie was angry and wouldn't speak to her, so they tended the geese until evening came and then went back.

Next morning, as they went out through the dark gateway, the princess said:

'Alas, Falada, you hang there!'

And Falada replied:

'Alas, you suffer grief and care.
If your mother only knew
Her heart would surely break in two.'

Outside the city, she sat down in the meadow again and began combing out her hair. Curdie came up and wanted to

snatch a couple of hairs, but she quickly said:

'Wind, wind, blow today,
Blow Curdie's hat away!
Make the boy run after it.
In the meantime here I'll sit
Combing out my hair and then
Braiding it all up again.'

Then the wind blew the hat off Curdie's head and far away, and he had to run after it. By the time he came back she had finished doing her hair, and he couldn't snatch a single hair. So they tended the geese until evening came and then went back.

That evening, however, when they were back in the city, Curdie went to the old king and said, 'I don't want to tend geese with that girl any longer.'

'Why not?' asked the old king.

'Oh, she bothers me all day long.'

The old king ordered him to say what she did. So Curdie said, 'When we take the flock of geese out through the dark gateway in the morning, there's a horse's head nailed to the wall, and she speaks to it and says:

"*Alas, Falada, you hang there!*"

Then the head replies:
"*Alas, you suffer grief and care.*
If your mother only knew
Her heart would surely break in two."'

And Curdie went on with his story, telling the old king what happened in the meadow where they took the geese out to pasture, and how he had to run after his hat in the wind.

The old king told him to go out again next day as usual, and when morning came he sat behind the dark gateway himself and heard the girl talking to Falada's head. Then he followed her out into the fields, and hid behind a bush in the meadow. Soon he saw for himself how the goose-girl and the gooseherd drove the flock of geese along, and after a while she sat down and unbraided her hair, which shone and gleamed. Next moment she repeated her verse:
'*Wind, wind, blow today,*
Blow Curdie's hat away!
Make the boy run after it.
In the meantime here I'll sit
Combing out my hair and then
Braiding it all up again.'

Then a gust of wind rose and blew Curdie's hat away, and he had to run a long way after it, while the girl combed and braided her hair,

and the old king watched everything she did. After that he went back, unnoticed, and when the goose-girl returned in the evening he took her aside and asked why she did all this.

'I mustn't tell you,' she said. 'I mustn't tell my troubles to any living soul, because I swore under the open sky not to, and if I hadn't sworn that oath I would have lost my life.'

He insisted, and gave her no peace, but he couldn't get anything out of her. So he said, 'If you won't say anything to me, then tell your troubles to the iron stove there.' And he went away.

Then she crept into the iron stove, began weeping and wailing, poured her heart out to it and said, 'Here I sit, abandoned by one and all although I am a king's daughter, and a wicked chambermaid forced me to strip off my royal clothes. Now she's taken my place with my bridegroom, and I have to toil as a goose-girl. If my mother only knew, her heart would surely break in two.'

However, the old king was standing outside close to the stovepipe, listening, and he heard what she said. Then he came in again and told her to get out of the stove. Royal clothes were put on her, and it was wonderful to see how beautiful she looked.

The old king sent for his son and told him he had the wrong bride: she was only a chambermaid, he said, but here was the real bride, who had once been a goose-girl. The prince was delighted when he saw how beautiful and good she was, and all the king's courtiers and close friends were invited to a great banquet. The bridegroom sat at the head of the table with the princess on one side of him and the chambermaid on the other, but the chambermaid was dazzled by

the glittering jewels the princess wore and didn't recognise her.

When they had eaten and drunk and were merry, the old king asked the chambermaid a riddle. What would a woman deserve, he said, if she had deceived her master in such-and-such a way? And he told the whole story of the goose-girl and her maid. Then he asked, 'What would your judgement on that woman be?'

To this the false bride replied, 'She deserves no better than to be stripped stark naked and put in a barrel with sharp nails on the inside, and two white horses should be harnessed to it to drag her from street to street until she dies.'

'That woman is you,' said the old king. 'You have passed judgement on yourself, and the sentence shall be carried out.'

And when it had been done, the young prince married his true bride, and they ruled their kingdom in peace and happiness.

__Translator's note:__ This famous story is one of those that Dorothea Viehmann gave the Grimm brothers. It contains many lingering traces of pre-Christian magical beliefs, particularly to do with horses, when the talking horse Falada still speaks to the persecuted heroine after his head has been cut off. The princess herself is able to cast spells to conjure up the wind. A belief in the binding power of a promise, even when it was extracted from her by force — it is safe enough for her to tell it to the stove, but not directly to any human being — is also a theme surrounded by mystery from the distant past.

Hansel and Gretel

Once upon a time there was a poor woodcutter who lived in a wretched little hovel in the forest with his wife and two children. The children were called Hansel and Gretel, and as they were a growing boy and girl the poor people needed more and more bread. Times were very difficult too, and all food was expensive, so the two parents were in great trouble.

One evening, when they had gone to their hard bed, the woodcutter sighed, 'Oh, wife, how are we going to keep the children fed this winter, when we don't have enough to eat ourselves?'

And the mother replied, 'All I can think of is for you to take them out into the forest, and the sooner the better, give each of them a little piece of bread, light them a fire, commend them to the care of the good Lord God, and leave them there.'

'Oh, dear heavens! How can I do such a thing to my own children, wife?' asked the woodcutter in dismay.

'Very well then, don't!' said the woman angrily. 'You might as well make a coffin for all four of us and watch the children die of hunger!'

The two children, who were still awake in their little bed of moss because they were so hungry, heard what their mother and father were saying to each other, and the little sister began to cry. But Hansel comforted her and said, 'Don't cry, Gretel. I'll think of something to help us.' He waited until his parents were asleep, stole out of the hovel, collected some little white pebbles in the moonlight and hid them well. Then he slipped indoors again, and soon he and his sister were asleep.

Next morning the parents carried out their plan. Their mother gave each of the children a piece of bread, saying, 'This is all the food there is for today, so go carefully with it.' Gretel carried the bread, Hansel secretly took his pebbles with him, their father had his axe for chopping wood, their mother locked up the house and followed with a jug of water. Hansel came behind his mother, so that he was walking along the path behind the others. He kept looking back at the hovel, and when he couldn't see it any more he dropped a white pebble, and then another a few steps a little later, and so on.

Now they were all in the middle of the deep forest, and the father made a fire. The children collected plenty of brushwood for it, and their mother said, 'You must be tired. Lie down by the fire and sleep while we cut wood, and we'll come back later and fetch you.'

The children slept for a little while, and when they woke up the sun was high in the sky, the fire had burnt out, and as Hansel and Gretel were hungry they ate their little slices of bread. However, their parents didn't come back. And after the children had slept again until it was dark, and they were still alone, Gretel began to cry and feel afraid. But Hansel comforted her, saying, 'Never fear, sister, the good Lord is with us. The moon will soon rise and then we'll go home.'

Sure enough, soon the moon rose in all its glory, lighting the children's way home as it shone on the silvery white pebbles. Hansel took Gretel's hand, and so the children walked on with each other, fearing nothing and with no further mishaps, and as day began to dawn they saw their father's roof through the bushes, came back to the little hovel in the forest, and knocked on the door. When their mother opened it and saw the children, she got a great fright and didn't know whether to be glad or to scold them, but their father was happy, and so the children were welcomed back into the little house.

But it wasn't long before the family ran short of food once more, and the parents talked to each other again and decided to take the children into the forest and leave them there in the care of heaven. Once again the children heard this sad discussion, and were heavy-hearted, but clever Hansel got up to go and look for more shiny pebbles. However, the door of the little house in the forest was locked, because his mother knew what he had done before, so she had made sure the door was well closed. But Hansel comforted his weeping little sister again, and said, 'Don't cry, dear Gretel. The good Lord knows all the paths in the world and will lead us to the right one.'

They all had to get up early next morning and go out into the forest again. Once more the children were given pieces of bread, though they were even smaller than the first time, and the way led yet deeper into the forest. However, Hansel was secretly crumbling his bread in his pocket, and he scattered it along the path instead of pebbles, thinking that the crumbs would show him and his little sister the way back. Everything happened just as it did before: the parents lit a big fire, the children had to sleep by it, and when they woke up they were alone and their parents didn't come back. Midday came, and Gretel shared her piece of bread with Hansel, because his had been crumbled up and was lying along the way they had come. Then they went to sleep again, and woke in the evening still forsaken and alone. Gretel cried, but Hansel trusted in God and felt sure the breadcrumbs would show them the way back. He waited until the moon had risen, and then took Gretel's hand and said, 'Come along, sister, it's time to go home.'

But when he looked for the crumbs there wasn't one to be seen, for the little birds in the forest had pecked them all up and made a good meal of them. So the children wandered through the forest all night and soon lost their way. They didn't know where they were, and felt very downcast. At last they went to sleep on some soft moss, and at dawn they woke up feeling very hungry, for they hadn't a morsel of bread left, and had to satisfy their hunger and thirst with the delicious woodland berries they found here and there.

As they were wandering around in the forest, with no idea where they were, a snow-white bird came flying along. It kept flying ahead of the children as if it wanted to show them the way, and they happily followed the bird. Suddenly they saw a little house. The bird flew up on its roof and started pecking at it. When the children came really close, they were overjoyed and amazed, for the little house had walls made of bread, the roof was thatched with pancakes, and the windows had panes of transparent sugar-candy. The children were very happy, and ate some of the roof of the little house, and part of a broken window-pane.

Then they suddenly heard a voice inside saying:
'Nibble, nibble, mousie!
Who's nibbling at my housie?'

To which the children replied:
'The wind so wild,
Heaven's own child!'

and went on eating, because they had been very hungry, and the house tasted wonderful.

Then the door of the little house opened, and out came an ancient, hump-backed little old woman with watery eyes. She was very ugly. Her face and forehead were all wrinkled, and in the middle of her face there was a great big nose. Her eyes were green as grass. The children were very scared, but the old woman seemed very friendly and said, 'Oh, dear children, come along into my house, do come in! I have much better cakes indoors!'

So the children were happy to follow the old woman, and once they were inside she gave them wonderful things to eat, everything the heart might desire, biscuits and marzipan, sugar and milk, apples and nuts, and delicious cakes. And while the children went on eating cheerfully, the old woman made them up two little beds with fine down pillows and lily-white linen sheets, where she put them to sleep.

They thought they were in heaven, said their evening prayers like good devout children, and went to sleep at once.

But the old woman was not what she seemed. She was a nasty, wicked witch who fattened up the children she lured into her little house of bread and cakes, and then ate them. That was what she meant to do to Hansel and Gretel. Early in the morning the witch, delighted with her catch, was standing by the bed where the children were still sleeping sweetly. She seized Hansel, pulled him out of bed, and carried him to the goose-pen, which had bars set close together round it, stuffing a gag into his mouth to prevent him from screaming. Then she shook poor Gretel awake, shouting roughly, 'Get up, you lazy thing! Your brother's in the goose-pen. We must cook him a good meal to make him nice and fat, and then I shall have a tasty roast boy to eat!'

Gretel was terrified and wept and wailed, but it was no use, she had to do as the witch said, get up, help to cook the meal and then carry it out to the shed herself, and weep with her imprisoned brother. The old woman thought nothing much of Gretel herself. Things went on like this for some time, and the witch often went out to the goose-pen and told Hansel to put a finger out through the bars, so that she could feel it and see if he was getting fat. However, Hansel always stuck a dry bone out, and she was surprised that he stayed so thin in spite of the good food he was eating. In the end she was tired of waiting, and told Gretel, 'Never mind, we'll roast him today.' She lit a roaring fire in the oven that stood beside her little house, and then put some loaves in to bake, so that she would have fresh bread to eat with her meat. Gretel was at her wits' end. At last the old witch told her to sit on the end of the bread-shovel and look into the oven, saying she would just push it a little way in so that Gretel could see if the loaves were nice and brown. But really she planned to roast the poor little girl before her brother.

Then the snow-white bird came flying along, singing, 'Take care, take care, beware, beware!' And Gretel's eyes were opened. She saw through the old woman's wicked trick, and said, 'Show me how to do it first, and then I will.'

The old woman immediately sat on the bread-shovel, and Gretel took the handle and pushed the shovel right into the oven. Then she slammed the little iron door, pushed the bolt over it, and as the oven were already red-hot the old witch was roasted inside it and died miserably. That was her reward for her wicked deeds. As for Gretel, she ran to Hansel, let him out of the goose-pen, and he came out and flung his arms round his faithful little sister's neck. They kissed, wept for joy, and gave thanks to God.

Then the white bird came back, with many other forest birds. They flew up to the pancake roof of the little house, where there was a nest, and each bird took a glowing jewel or a pearl out of it and carried it down to the children. Gretel held out her apron to take all the precious stones, and the snow-white bird sang:

'Jewels and pearls we pay
For breadcrumbs on our way.'

So the children knew that the little birds were grateful for the breadcrumbs that Hansel had scattered on the path. Then the white bird flew ahead of them again to show them the way out of the forest. But soon they came to a great river, and there they stood unable to go any further, for they couldn't get across. However, a large and beautiful swan suddenly came swimming up and the children called, 'Lovely swan, there you float – carry us over like a boat.' And the swan bent its long neck, swam to the children and took them over to the opposite bank, one after the other. The white bird had already flown across, and kept flying ahead of the children until they finally came out of the forest and saw their parents' house.

The old woodcutter and his wife were sitting in their little hovel, sad and silent, grieving for the children, regretting a thousand times over that they had let them go, and sighing, 'Oh, if only Hansel and Gretel would come back, just once, we would never leave them alone in the forest again!' At that moment the door opened, though no one had knocked on it, and in came Hansel and Gretel themselves! What rejoicings there were! And the joy was even greater when the children showed the pearls and precious stones they had brought home with them, so now there was an end to the family's poverty, and they never went short of anything again.

Translator's note: This version of the story is by Ludwig Bechstein, born in 1801, who borrowed or retold many of the Grimms' tales. His German Fairy Tale Book was even more popular than the Grimms' collection when it was first published in 1845. His 'Hansel and Gretel' hardly differs at all from the story as told by the Grimms, who had it from Wilhelm's future wife Dorothea Wild. The Grimms could not quite decide whether to say that it is a mother or a stepmother who tries to lose the children in the forest; Ludwig Bechstein has no qualms in making her their real mother.

First published by Carl Hanser Verlag München Wien 2004
First published in Great Britain by Egmont UK Limited in 2006
239 Kensington High Street, London W8 6SA

Illustrations copyright © Henriette Sauvant 2004
Translation copyright © Anthea Bell 2006

ISBN-10 1 4052 1832 0 (Hardback)
ISBN-13 978 1 4052 1832 0 (Hardback)
ISBN-10 1 4052 2702 8 (Paperback)
ISBN-13 978 1 4052 2702 5 (Paperback)

2 4 6 8 10 9 7 5 3 1

A CIP catalogue record for this title is available from the British Library

Printed and bound in Singapore